twentynine palms

twentynine palms   daniel pyne

A Novel

■ COUNTERPOINT BERKELEY

Library of Congress Cataloging-in-Publication Data

Pyne, Daniel.
Twentynine Palms : a novel / by Daniel Pyne.
p. cm.
ISBN-13: 978-1-58243-573-2
ISBN-10: 1-58243-573-1
1. California, Southern—Fiction. 2. Noir fiction. I. Title.

PS3616.Y56T84 2010
813'.6—dc22

2010005454

Interior design by Elyse Strongin, Neuwirth & Associates, Inc.
Cover design by Ann Weinstock

COUNTERPOINT
2117 Fourth Street
Suite D
Berkeley, CA 94710

www.counterpointpress.com
Distributed by Publishers Group West

10 9 8 7 6 5 4 3 2 1

For Joan. Always.

twentynine palms

prologue

■

a.

Imagine a perfect square of impossibly blue sky.

Darkness frames it; a handmade ladder of two-by-fours reaches into it.

It could be Heaven.

The boy has butterflies in his stomach, and an urge to turn back. He knows, somehow, that if he climbs up into the sunlight, nothing will ever be quite the same.

Fourteen-year-old Tory Geller waits upstairs in the master bedroom of this half-finished California-Ranch-Mission-Tudor-Mediterranean-whatthefuck tract home, sitting in the yawning gap where doors with modest pan-European ambitions will someday be hung. Tory is cocksure and cool. His legs dangle over the hardscape twenty feet below and he smokes and gazes out across the cheerful clutter of downtown Santa Barbara, to the slate-water harbor and the smear of Channel Islands hanging just above the ocean horizon.

"You better've brought something." Tory says this with sharpness, doesn't turn.

Behind him, Jack Baylor, also fourteen, steps off the construction ladder and out of the stairless stairwell. Smaller than Tory, still growing, Jack wears thick glasses and a gold-and-blue St. Stevens Day Camp windbreaker with frayed elastic cuffs. A green glass bottle of Mickey's Big Mouth beer comes out of one pocket of his jacket, Oreos from the other, and Jack lays his offerings down on the plywood subfloor next to Tory.

"So," Jack says, diving in, "like. Tory, hey. I'm really sorry about this whole deal with Cathy—"

Tory opens the Mickey's and takes a noisy swallow.

"—it's just, my mom knows her mom from church, the thing's a setup," Jack pleads his case. "I mean, like I even want to fucking go to the stupid dance." Not bad. He's added the "fucking" at the last minute, nice touch, flinty and hard-assed, he hopes.

Tory belches. "You swipe this brew?"

Jack's face reddens. There is nothing in his mind now besides this wholly blind desire to purchase Tory's respect. But, here, at fourteen, Jack has not yet perfected his lies. "No."

"Wuss." Tory smokes, belches, drinks.

Wuss. Jack waits, and wonders what will happen next. His friends have warned him that Tory might just beat the shit out of him. Jack has never been in a fight.

"You gonna stand there all day?" Tory says. Jack sits—safely distant in case Tory gets an itch to shove him off the edge. Tory's nostrils spill smoke dismissively. "Relax, Baylor. N.B.D. Know what I'm saying? Hell. Sutton's already done her."

Done her. Jack knows what this means. Nods gravely.

Tory smokes. He looks sidelong at Jack. "Sutton says she got both his balls in her mouth, at the same time."

This, to Jack, sounds wrong. He wrestles with a mental picture of shy-but-perky Cathy DeLong, varsity football Peppette, vaguely arranged ass-up and head south between the splayed hairy legs of the pothead, Tommy Sutton. "Is that good?" he wonders, aloud.

A geyser of beer spews from Tory's mouth. He's laughing. After a worried moment, Jack joins in, slowly convincing himself that he meant it to be funny.

"All right."

"Yeah."

"Yeah. Yeah."

Tory offers Jack the crooked cigarette. Jack accepts, slips it between his dry lips, but doesn't smoke. His mouth is cotton. Tory swigs the Mickey's and considers the ocean again.

After what he believes to be a reasonable interval, Jack tries to give the cigarette back. Tory waves it away. "All yours, man."

"I . . . no, better not. My, you know, mom. If she gets a whiff, on my breath—"

Tory holds up an Oreo. "What do you think these are for? Kills the stink completely."

In point of fact, Jack thought the cookies were for when Tory got hungry. But he keeps the cigarette. Puffs and puffs and puffs without inhaling, nevertheless beginning to feel kind of tingly and sick. The Mickey's drained, Tory throws it down into a pile of scrap lumber below, where the jade glass shatters.

"You know what's on those islands?" Tory is pointing west, into the haze.

"Goats." Jack did a report on the Channel Islands in fourth grade. "Sheep, sea lions, seals, gulls, fossils."

Tory looks disappointed. For a moment Jack wonders if Tory

wanted to tell him this himself, or did Tory, in fact, believe that there was something else out there?

"But at some point," Jack continues, "somebody brought all these goats out there, and they let them go wild—" Tory's bored already, but Jack's in too deep, he has to finish— "and they just kept breeding and breeding and now there's thousands of wild goats and nobody knows what to do with them. It's messed up. Sometimes they let people go out and hunt them and junk."

Tory shrugs. "Yeah, well I know for a fact there's frat guys that go out there and, you know, fuck the goats. Part of the initiation."

Jack's horror and speculation prevent him (oh Jesus) from processing Tory's subsequent spare but graphic (goats!) recitation of this apparently long-standing UCSB Greek system sacrament.

"Oh, man," Jack says, when Tory finishes. "Who told you that?"

"I get things here and there. You know. And what I know, man—well, I know what really goes on. It's like, they teach you one thing. But what really goes on? Is something else."

Wind comes through the house like an emotion, filling it with an easy silence, pushing paper scraps around in corners and sifting the sawdust.

"The guys all said you were gonna kill me," Jack confesses.

"Which guys?"

"You know—some of the guys—" Jack hesitates, sensing a misstep here, accidental betrayal in the making. Will Tory kill *them*?

"—Christ, they're such pussies," Tory says.

Jack's empty grin, like a lawn jockey's, cuts cold and meaningless.

"They don't get it," Tory is saying, "they're full of shit. It comes down to one thing and one thing only."

Jack wonders: What? What one thing?

"You know."

"Yeah."

"I mean, hey. Girls'll come, and girls'll go. But you and me—?" Tory deliberately leaves the sentence hanging there, looking at Jack, without expression, as if the completion of his thought is so obvious as to be unnecessary, as if it's implicit.

And Jack nods, pretending he knows, fourteen in full, confounded, confirmed, content. He gazes out across the lazy green ramble of the seaside city he has always known to be home.

Out toward a colorless ocean, and the vague, private islands of goats.

b.

Shapes, slender whale-grey phantasms, stumble from the foaming tide.

Surfers.

The roar of a storm-swelled ocean thunders low from the marine layer beyond them.

Black with bits of winter-white flesh, unzipped wet suits, hoods flapping behind them like weird rubber cowls of some long-submerged Benedictine order, the taller of the two young men is hauling his gasping companion to the shallows of Rincon Beach.

Tory and Jack are twenty.

"Little cocksucking Valley shit fucking cut me off!" Tory barks. Jack eases his friend down, then runs back to chase their long boards before they float away.

By the time Jack returns with their sticks, Tory is spitting seawater and blinking the salt and sand out of his eyes. "Goddamn it! They shouldn't even fucking be out here!"

"He's a pup. They're Valley pups. Forget about it." Jack drags the surfboards beyond the reach of the tide. "You're welcome, by the way. Thank God for Junior Lifesaving, huh?"

"Never took it."

Farther up the beach, where clumps of clothes and towels and flip-flops are waiting, Jack strips down the top of his wet suit. Tory glares back at the water. Three more surfers are coming in. Day-Glo stripes on high-fashion wet suits, they're barely teenagers. Sun-bleached hair. Poolside San Fernando Valley tans, Calabasas or Woodland Hills.

"I'm only saying. Somebody should explain the concept to those guys."

"There's a concept?"

"Priority. Do not drop in on another man's wave. The surfer who is closest to the breaking wave has priority."

"He was already up."

"Because he jumped my line."

"Since when have you ever cared about the rules?"

"Fuck you."

"Maybe you should've let a geek have his ride. Take the next wave. You knew he was gonna bail, Tory."

"These are my waves."

"Your waves."

"Yeah."

"Your ocean."

"That is correct." Tory starts to walk toward the three surfers. Amiable: "I just want to explain the concept to this dickhead."

Jack turns his back, on Tory and the ocean. Picks up his towel and begins to dry off. He feels a chill, but not the kind you get from cold air. He knows what's coming. He tries not to think about what his options are.

Tory intercepts the three surfers down the beach as they come

out of the water. They've seen him coming. The smallest kid puts
a hand up, a gesture of genuine apology. Without any warning,
Tory attacks him. Every punch connects, vicious.

Jack rubs the towel in his thick hair. The roar of the surf over-
powers the sound of feet splashing in shallow tidal water, fists
slapping skin, the kid's screams for help. Dropping his towel,
Jack wraps his clothes together and puts them on his board to
keep them clear of the sand. He doesn't want to look. If he can't
hear it, and he doesn't see it, does it exist? A smoldering sun flares
hot behind Jack's head for an instant, lending him a sudden, dim
halo. He feels its heat. He cannot stop himself. He looks.

What he sees down-beach, in the water, of course, requires
him to run.

He reaches Tory and pulls him away from the gasping teen-
ager whose eyes are already swollen red, shut, a pink slick of
blood from split lips draining down his chin and neck and hair-
less, baby-fat chest.

Tory's fury turns. He lashes out blindly, screaming incoher-
ently, the gist of which suggests Jack mind his own fucking
business, which—in an instant—Jack knows is good advice
because Tory's wildly thrown, bone-hard fist connects with the
side of Jack's head and a pain of molten shrieking sharpness
splits through Jack's eye and buries itself deep inside his skull.
His body twists, dissolves, nausea washing over him, and he
vomits into the water.

Now the Valley dudes are hauling their bloody companion
away, and Jack is stumbling backward, and Tory, defused, is
looking on in surprise, as if he just happened upon an accident.
Jack's thoughts in this moment are incredibly clear on one point:
something bad has happened something bad has happened something bad has bad has bad has happened—has—has—

"Jack—hold still—let me look at it—"

"Oh Jesusfuck oh—"

"Jack—"

"Get away from me!"

"Jack—"

"Owshitowshitowshitshitshit—"

"Jack, will you let me look at your eye? Shit—here—sorry—but what is fucking wrong with you? You know? Don't ever do that. Don't ever try to—"

"Get out. Of my way."

Then, Tory, seeing it: "Oh man. Oh fuck."

What.

"Here put this—at least it's—you just don't—don't do that, Jack, you just don't—"

And Jack has never felt this kind of pain before and never will again, and never will shake the memory of the dull, black, searing screw someone is bearing down on, driving deep beneath the socket of his eye. All he can think about is the pain. Tory's voice is distant, something overheard.

"It's not bleeding. It's okay."

They're moving. Up the beach. The sand, on the soles of his feet, burns.

"I'll drive."

Jack looks up into the sun. It burns through the haze, and bleaches everything

white.

c.

Now, a woman, improbably beautiful, coiled naked in the low hills of a white down duvet, waits for Jack, hopes crashing. Her platinum hair is tangled, her face flushed from lovemaking just minutes ago, eyes liquid, thighs slick. She's three weeks past forty.

A toilet flushes. Watching him come out from the bathroom and circle the bed, Hannah's face is willfully empty of emotion, as if to suggest it doesn't matter what Jack does now, which only underlines the utter desperation that overtakes her despite the Ativan she popped as soon as he uncoupled and rolled out of bed.

Golf tees spill, scatter across the red Spanish pavers from the pocket of his shorts. He gropes for them. "Shit."

"Don't worry about it. Rosaria will clean up in here later." Hannah stretches out, her breasts, nearly perfect spheres, levitating, defying all Newton's laws of gravity. "Unless you can't afford to waste the tees. Do you need money?" Then she covers her mouth, as if coy. "Oops. Sorry. Oh, Hannah, you castrating little slut."

He smiles mechanically, pulls the baggy shorts up his legs, in a hurry, buttons them, feeling once again the urgent need to get out. White polo shirt. High-tech huaraches.

"I didn't mean it." Her voice reaches for him, clutches at him. He's got to walk out now. "Shit. I'm not good at this part. Listen, baby, what if we—" She stops, he's looking back at her. "No," she realizes. Tears well in her eyes. "No."

Tears, from cold blue eyes.

He leans down and kisses her forehead lightly before he walks out.

Jack is thirty-five.

It's the year of the Rat.

Later, in his apartment, Jack's face, like the rest of him, is glazed with sweat from the midday L.A. heat.

His eyes are closed. Only one of them needs to be. He is blind if he opens the wrong one, but that seldom happens and he doesn't think about it. A world of diminished perspective is, for

Jack, status quo. Colors explode against the inside of his eyelid, blossom with the hum of an electric fan. Damp tendrils of his hair tremble in the machine-made breeze.

A phone is ringing.

Jack's eyes open. He waits.

He's pretty sure it's Hannah.

Calculating: she would still be in bed. He smells her perfume, Vera Wang, mixed with the residue of their recent, workmanlike act of copulation. It's a smell, he decides, that is more than a little unpleasant.

The phone rings, and rings, and rings.

An off-key beep, followed by a moment of silence, then a freakishly compressed voice surges through the cheap speaker of the answering machine.

"Jack?" Jack doesn't move. "Hey, Jack, it's Tory. Are you there, man? Jack?" Tory. Shit. "You left your cell phone here."

Shit.

"Must've been, I don't know, yesterday? And you didn't fucking notice? I mean, hell, what kind of actor are you, Jack? I mean, yo, it's kind of like that joke about the actor who comes home, his wife's been raped by his agent, his kids sold into white slavery, his house burned to the ground, and the guy's like, 'My agent came to my house?'" Tory laughs, then lapses into silence. Expecting Jack to pick up, irritated that he doesn't. A short, frustrated intake of breath: "Okay. Anyway. Your phone's here. Call me. I'm home."

Dial tone. Silence. Jack closes his eyes again. Cell phone. Fuck. Goddamn it. Shit.

He imagines the Hope Ranch house, sun through the French doors, Tory standing in the middle of the cavernous ballroom, holding Jack's cheap Nokia like it's some kind of radioactive waste, his eyes dead, pretty and mean in the way married money will spoil the flesh and rot the soul. When Tory's short fuse is lit, the slender muscles of his neck will tighten and relax, tighten and relax.

Wondering about Jack's fucking phone.

Jack could have left it. That's possible. Not yesterday, but Tuesday, when he was last up there, helping Tory clean out the Montecito garage before the old house went on the market. But two days had passed. Tory is right. It's inconceivable Jack wouldn't know his phone was gone.

A dull, tingling, vacant rolling dread gathers in Jack's chest, slow crawling, connected to nothing, borne of the boy's unknown, the boy's unknowable, and the immutable yearning for acceptance by that which can never give it. Tory was Jack's event horizon, and, once inside his gravitational pull, falling into the black hole was a certainty. That they have remained friends is as baffling to Jack as the compressed planes of his halved vision. And what has happened with Hannah is so primal that Jack knows, has known from the beginning, it would, must, inevitably catalyze a spectacular meltdown.

Jack doesn't, however, regret what he's done.

His mind calculates. If he'd left the phone at Tory's on Tuesday, not today after fucking Hannah (twice) at noon and then telling her the affair was over—if he'd really left the phone on Tuesday while cleaning the old house and discovered it missing when he got back to L.A. and didn't know where it was or where he'd left it and wasn't patient enough to retrace his steps since he was, say, waiting for a call from his agent—couldn't Jack simply have replaced it? Visit a T-Mobile store, buy a new calling plan, get the free RAZR. After all, Jack had been talking about giving Verizon the shitcan for months because he kept losing the signal on Olympic between Roxbury and McCarthy Vista, a vortex of wireless cross-cancellation so frustrating that a few of Jack's other actor friends had stopped driving the Olympic corridor altogether.

Jack has a new phone. Which is why he didn't realize (or care) that the old one was at Tory's. Which explains everything except why it was in the master bedroom. Well, Rosario could have found it and put it there, not knowing whose it was, which works, until Tory asks Rosario—

—or Jack could just talk to Hannah and she—

—no, talking to Hannah would—

—talking to Hannah wouldn't—

—talking with Hannah, Jesus—

—but, nevertheless, the thing with the new phone is solid. Who the hell knows how it got upstairs into the bedroom (if that was, in fact, where Tory found it)? Jack will go out now and get a new one, go right to the store, now, and get a new one—

—or just go—

—go—

—gone.

And Tory? Tory, after racking the cordless house phone in its cradle, will cross his cavernous foyer and hurry up his wide stone staircase, past the broken remains of Jack's Nokia along the baseboard of the upstairs hallway not far from the dent in the hand-trowelled plaster where it hit and exploded after Tory fastballed it from the bedroom, their grand white master bedroom, where everything is slightly in disarray, women's clothes scattered, bed unmade, the single golf tee Jack missed and Tory will find, under the bed, behind the corner of the duvet.

He'll walk to a carved set of double doors salvaged from some foreclosed Oaxacan hacienda, and open them, to stare inside at the Italian marble tile tomb his wife modestly calls their master bathroom. Faint pink tendrils swirl in the tepid water of the massive tub each time another drop plummets from the flat-mouthed Italian spigot.

And like a commuter looking at a traffic accident from a passing car, Tory's expression will never change. He'll pull the tub drain, use the fluffy white bath towels to wipe the basin, drop the same towels on the marble floor and mop up the motley pattern of overlapping, bloody-wet shoeprints the EMTs left in the course of their recent visit, using his foot to push the towels around.

On the antique dresser is the teak brush from Fiji that Tory's mother gave him for his tenth birthday. Tory will brush his hair, worried that it seems thinner than yesterday, possibly irritated by the prospect of early male pattern baldness when Jack's hair is, no question, healthier and thicker and in no danger of leaving. Tory will brush his hair serenaded by the vacant thrum of the tub draining.

Jack, however, will only know that Tory called.

one

■

The merciless heat.

The whine of tires on asphalt, growing louder, louder, louder, loud.

A blue belly lizard charges up out of a rivulet creasing the pebbles of the shoulder, skitters to the broken line of white paint that splits the black road in two. It cranes its neck, head jerking up and down, jowls flaring, its tiny heart pumping wildly, its eyes narrow slits of fierce darkness and abject fear. The girl who sent the lizard running walks past, feet scuffing pebbles, her path taking her tight along the shoulder of the road. She doesn't see the lizard. She's fourteen, overheated, not really pretty yet, sundress, spandex, Day-Glo zinc oxide striped on her nose and cheeks like war paint.

Her icy blue eyes squint to study the horizon, hopeful, behind egg-shaped sunglasses. The heat comes up through the soles of her Converse All-Stars and sears her feet. She shifts the small Hello Kitty backpack to her other shoulder and takes a swallow from her big bottle of purified water.

Mechanical bumblebee sounds buzz from her backpack. Reaching to a side pocket and finding a flip phone, she has to cup her hand and shade the screen to read the text:

heyyyysup?

The salutation and question. Small fingers flick across the keypad of the phone and text back:

ssdd.

Same stuff, different day.

She senses the car behind her before she hears it. She turns around, legs still pushing her east.

What seems only a mirage—a dazzling black cartoon car— suddenly materializes out of the shimmering puddle of heat distortion on the highway horizon and hovers over it, growing quickly larger. Blaring rock-and-roll music from open windows, the car, a Buick sedan, races forward, at, then directly over and past, the blue belly, its life spared by a miracle of time and place.

The lizard tumbles wildly in the wake of the car, fifty, sixty feet down-highway. Its tail separates from its body, a useless tactic of survival that here only serves to cheat the creature of future mobility, and probably hasten its surrender to the food chain.

Thumb out, the girl watches the Buick whip past her, tossing her hair and dress around. No brake lights, it's not stopping. She smoothes her dress, fixes her hair, keeps walking.

Her bumblebee ring tone offers comfort:

wysiwyg.

What you see is what you get.

A falcon swoops across the highway, catches the blue belly in its talons, and soars again gracefully out over the brown desert. The lizard thrashes desperately, and in doing so executes itself on the point of a sharp talon.

The girl never sees it, walking and texting:
iyss.
If you say so. And then, an afterthought:
icbw.
It could be worse.
The falcon settles lightly on the top of a broken knob of rock, high on the hill above the highway, and eats a late lunch in the afternoon sun.
r u ok?
gr8. 404. nbd.
kewl.
yup.
The screen indicates no service. The battery icon flashes, low. She folds the phone and puts it away.

A few miles west, on either side of the highway, modular slant-roofed homes squat defiantly on their parceled acres of Mojave Desert. Fierce-looking, wind-whipped zealots with rusted TV aerials for hats, they wait for the God of Fast Food Chains and Mini-malls to send property values skyrocketing, or for the Big Earthquake to put them out of their misery. Higher up, in the ragged hills among giant, broken, burnt-orange boulders turned bloody by the sun, the larger stucco tract homes with industrial air-conditioning and polarized windows and upside-down loans gaze back emptily at traffic that hurries past as if embarrassed.

Joshua trees, thick and spiny thugs with multiple arms held aloft, swarm in from the south in an outrage at the invasion of men; tens of thousands of trees storming the interlopers' highway and then retreating into the barren, scraped-out, labyrinthine valleys to the north, where the poor subsist, and the wealthy hide their multi-million-dollar desert homes, and where, at the end of a rutted road, Tory Geller and his wife Hannah have thirty-five acres and a purposefully crooked house designed by a famous young Chinese architect.

Inexplicably, just beyond the RESUME 55 speed-limit sign that establishes the eastern boundary of Joshua Tree city proper, the horde stops short, as if what lies ahead, in Twentynine Palms, discourages it. The only Joshua tree in Twentynine Palms is planted in the asphalt courtyard of the Rancho Del Dorotea motel, right next to the bleached turquoise swimming pool.

Jack cannot see it from his balcony.

The balcony in Room 203 looks west, to the lurching litter of civilization that is Joshua Tree and Yucca Valley, strung together like cheap plastic jewelry along Highway 62. It makes Jack smile.

He considers the dying day, and the lights beginning to glow across the desert, and for a moment he can't remember why he's here. Sometimes the world is clear to Jack; sometimes it's an impenetrable abstract of shapes, colors, vectors, and emotions, strange values and stranger contrast.

His shirt is soaked through. The rasping of crickets soothes him. From his pocket he takes a pack of filterless cigarettes, then a platinum lighter, fires up and smokes, holding the cigarette between his thumb and forefinger like a movie star. After a moment, he balances the cigarette ash-up on the balcony railing, and starts to unbutton his shirt.

Inside, the air-conditioning control knob is broken off, stuck on the highest setting, blowing frigid air, while the open balcony door blows desert heat. Jack strips to the bathing suit he's been wearing since he left Los Angeles. There are those thin, abrasive motel towels in the bathroom. He finishes his cigarette, flicks it off the balcony in a shower of ash, then closes both doors and walks down the stairs to the pool to take up residence under the solitary Joshua tree, on a vinyl-woven chaise that is almost brand-new.

For a few minutes he's still hurtling down the highway. With his eyes closed Jack can feel the speed, conjure landscapes to flicker past in his peripheral vision.

Slowly, his body sinks into the warm plastic webbing, and he brakes. A liquid heat washes him. He arranges the towel over his eyes, inhales the pungent smell of industrial laundering and disinfectant. The setting sun scrapes its hot needles across his skin. Now, finally, perhaps he will sleep.

"Zach. Zachary, don't you go in the deep end!"

Splashing sounds bring Jack to consciousness under the towel. He's missed sunset, and the desert sky glows cobalt blue. Pale orange neon lights that rim the eaves of the motel are sputtering to life.

Jack adjusts the towel. The water in the pool at his feet is choppy, someone in it, splashing.

"If you go into that end, young man, we're going back inside." A woman's voice ricochets, hollow, around the concrete courtyard, followed by more splashing, and a child's imitation of an outboard motor. Lips to water.

"Zach—"

Jack doesn't look up. He doesn't need to. He paints a mental picture of the pale, plump woman with jet-black perm standing flaccid-thighed in plus-size swimwear at the end of the pool, glowering as her little tyke flails his way toward the five-foot mark, deaf to her threats. Former high-school prom princess turned pumpkin, her lips flattened into a humorless slit. Foam flip-flops slap over wet concrete, water churns—

"Ooowww!"

"You heard me."

"That hurts!"

"Out."

"I could still touch bottom."

"Let's go."

The boy's reluctant, soggy footsteps recede into the shadows, and Jack sits up in time to catch the greenish-white, fleshy backs of a woman's legs as she leads her son toward a unit on the ground level, at the far end of the motel. Her white shorts gleam iridescent, lit from below by the pool lights.

What is Tory's theory? Something about women, marriage, children, the time bombs mothers plant deep inside their daughters; hard body spoilage, breasts drooping, butts dropping, faces inflating like bread dough, the tight hats of sensible hair, car pools, Botox, and the desperation. Jack rises from the chaise and leaps out over the pool, arching his back, knifing into the tepid water.

Opening his eyes to the sting of chlorine, Jack grazes the pool bottom with his stomach, and then lets his momentum bring him back slowly to the surface. The hot night air inexplicably gives him goose bumps.

Jack floats easily.

"I lost the sight in my left eye when I was twenty." Three gentle taps to the business end of Jack's unlit cigarette, then he spins it in his fingers, forestalling the inevitable trip outside to smoke it. "If you look close, the pupil is distorted. Like a teardrop. But I don't consider myself disabled or anything. I don't even think about it all that much anymore." Salisbury steak is the blue plate special, and Jack ordered his at the bar. "You adjust," Jack says, answering what he always assumes is the unasked question. "I'm supposed to wear glasses, clear lenses, for protection. Of the, you know, good eye." Jack is making conversation, enjoying the thrum of his own voice. "I don't know why I never have."

The lean bartender nods, cutting limes.

"I see like a camera. Everything's flat. Compressed. But if I move my head, slightly, like this," Jack shifts imperceptibly, "I'm taking two pictures, my mind compares them, measures the difference, and I get my sense of depth."

"Okay."

"At first it was hard, though."

"I know some soldiers, lost eyes in Iraq. They say they have trouble shaking hands. Parking the car. Chopsticks."

"Chopsticks are tough for everybody," Jack allows.

There are few customers tonight in the Roundup Room. Jack prefers the anonymity of his corner stool at the bar to the checkerboard-cloth-covered wagon-wheel tables for six and slide-in booths in the over-lit dining area. When was the last time, he wonders, there were six people having dinner together in here? Two couples, marines from the nearby combat training facility and their dates, are the only diners. The jarheads are having the all-you-can-eat popcorn shrimp, and their ketchup-splattered plates suggest it has become a how-much-will-they-cook situation. Three heat-jacked, love-shot, middle-aged gals sit in a booth with a pitcher of margaritas, sharing their perky loneliness. Another marine, older, in street clothes but with the unmistakable high-and-tight haircut, gunnery-sergeant set to his mouth, and intricate, indecipherable tattoos on both biceps, sits hunched at the opposite end of the bar from Jack, nursing a lite beer and occasionally glancing up, hopeful, at the door.

"I'll tell you what, though," Jack continues, unable, for some reason, to shut up, "it makes you greedy, about what you do see. It forces you to see more clearly. You don't waste your time on the visual garbage. A man with one eye wants to focus on the things that are worth seeing."

The bartender rolls out some more limes. "So I guess you spend your free time surfing porn sites on the web."

"He's a comedian," Jack says, smiling. Shut up, Jack tells himself. Shut up, go outside, have your smoke.

Salisbury steak with Brussels sprouts and cactus shavings is an attempt, Jack guesses, at nouvelle Western cuisine. He eats hungrily, without thinking about it. It's his first meal since an Egg McMuffin and Diet Coke breakfast, on the grey, fog-bound road back from Santa Barbara at dawn.

For a moment he wonders if he dreamed it.

"Been out here before?" The bartender is bored. Just grinding through another shift.

"I've got this friend, married a swimsuit model. She's filthy rich and they've got a house in the north hills. Usually I stay up there."

"Not this time?"

"No."

"Swimsuit model. That's sweet." Jack pushes his plate back, politely trying to put a punctuation on the conversation, but, apropos of nothing, now the bartender waxes on: "Before he got married, my cousin Cody was, like, this major poozle hound. He had a theory that, before you get serious about a girl, you want to meet her mother. Seriously. Because, according to Cody, the mom is what she's going to look like when, you know, the fruit goes past ripe."

"Past ripe."

The bartender smiles. "Hey. Two pictures."

"What?"

"Two pictures, one eye. Like you were saying. It's the multiple pictures that give you the depth of perception."

"It's bullshit, though," Jack says. "Don't you think?"

The bartender shrugs, suddenly on the defensive for his cousin. "So, your friend, did he ever meet the swimsuit girl's mother?"

Jack thinks. "He did, yeah."

"And?"

There's a commotion in the kitchen. Raised voices, pans clattering. Everyone in the restaurant pretends not to notice. The bartender takes Jack's empty plate away and replaces it with a cup of coffee and brandy snifter filled with two fingers of Sambuca. Jack swirls the glass, trying to rinse a stray bean back down with its buddies.

Abruptly, the kitchen doorway bangs open, a lanky cook appears pushing ahead of him a sullen girl with a Hello Kitty backpack. He scolds her in Spanish, she says nothing, her Day-Glo sunscreen smeared across her cheeks, her unscreened arms sunburned painfully red. The girl just stares at her feet until the cook gets tired of yelling and goes back into the kitchen with a sense of finality.

"Hey."

The girl looks up and locks eyes with Jack.

"I'm Jack. What up?"

The front door opens and closes on Jack's blind side; Jack glances toward it out of habit, and discovers he can't stop looking at the young woman who enters, his breath literally caught for an instant in his chest before he remembers to breathe again, she's that pretty.

"Rachel," the Hello Kitty girl tells him, but Jack's not listening anymore.

Hitching up her short green dress, the woman lifts herself onto a bar stool halfway between Jack and the marine sergeant. Her legs cross gracefully to let one green high-heeled pump dangle. Then she takes it off, puts it up on the bar, and rubs her foot.

"These shoes are murdering me," she says. The bartender pours her a Wild Turkey straight up. "No wonder they call them Fuck Me pumps."

The bartender laughs. The young woman in the green dress manages to look around the entire room without making eye contact with Jack.

"I heard about a guy who makes a thing you can put in the heel to make them more comfortable," the bartender is saying.

"That's pretty vague. A guy? A thing?"

"Didn't occur to me to take notes."

"Ha ha."

"I thought you were going dancing in Victorville tonight."

"I thought this all-you-can-eat shrimp deal was supposed to draw customers."

"Talk to the boss, m'lady."

"Yeah. As if."

They both laugh.

Jack pretends to study the oil-swirls in his coffee, so she won't think he's staring. But he is, staring. The dim light that falls on her from old recessed spots softens her face to a pleasant blur of pinkish white framed by dark hair that folds to her shoulder. Smudges of mauve eye shadow, serious, impenetrable eyes. A slur of lavender lipstick betrays the sad smile.

One of the old gals, slender, white-haired, stands up with the empty margarita pitcher and brings it to the bar for a refill. Jack tap-taps his cigarette again.

"Excuse me. The girl who just came in—"

Both the bartender and white-haired woman glance at Jack, wondering if he's talking to them. Jack waits. The older woman smiles, self-conscious. Jack smiles back. The bartender refills the pitcher, delivers it, and looks at Jack. "Yes sir?"

"I'd like to buy her a drink."

"The girl?" The bartender's eyes shift to Rachel, still waiting, behind Jack, having so recently evaporated from his landscape that it takes him a second to realize where the misunderstanding could be.

"No, no—" Jack tilts his head toward the young woman in the green dress and meets the bartender's expressionless gaze with an easy smile.

The bartender tightens his lips. "Okay, one: don't call her a girl, she won't like it. And, two: you'll have to ask her first, because, as you may have keenly observed with your single eye, my friend, I know her and I don't want to piss her off. She's ferocious, when she gets pissed."

Jack blinks.

The older woman turns with her Margarita refill to go back to her friends. Her feet get tangled. She starts to fall. Jack reacts, grabs the pitcher—it sloshes, doesn't spill—and simultaneously catches her by the arm, gallant. The old gal's friends spontaneously applaud, delighted. Jack steadies the woman, hands her the pitcher.

"You all right?"

Blushing fiercely, she nods, "Fine. Yes. I'm—sorry. My feet . . ." Jack cuts his eyes toward the young woman in the green dress again, but discovers Rachel and her backpack sliding purposefully onto the stool beside him, directly in his line of sight.

"Rachel," she says.

"I know. I heard you the first time."

"Oh." She catches the bartender, "Hey, can I have some water, please?"

The bartender frowns, annoyed. "I have to charge you a dollar."

"For water?"

"Put it on my tab," Jack says.

The bartender looks at him a little irritably, and moves away to get a glass.

"Thanks." Rachel studies Jack for a moment, critically, as if he were a math problem, then picks at the nail polish on her thumb.

"Where are your parents, Rachel?"

"I'm not supposed to talk to strangers," she says in a rote monotone.

The marine sergeant slides heavily off his stool and walks over to the woman in the green dress, who stares straight ahead, measuring his approach in the mirror. Sipping her whiskey and shaking her head slightly in response to whatever the marine is asking her, she never stops smiling, even when the sergeant steps back, almost as if slapped, and runs his thick hand across the level playing field of his flattop. Regrouping, he asks something else. She turns to him, her whole body facing him, and talks to him kindly for a moment longer.

Jack watches this, his heart in his groin. And then, shamelessly, he commits himself, suddenly, predictably, to wanting this woman as much as he has ever wanted anything; to fold her into his arms, soothe the disappointment from her smile, to move into one of those slant-roofed shacks on two hundred acres of barren desert, homestead, depurate himself, court her, win her, earn her. Well, and sleep with her, yes, but—it plays out for him in fast-forward, like a Lifetime channel TV movie, and, Jack realizes with the usual tinge of disappointment, that it actually *was* a Lifetime movie, a ten-hankie chick flick in which he played the part of the foolish marine who never stood a chance.

Jack wants to sleep with her, and he knows from experience that he probably will, it's just a matter of mechanics now. The real sergeant has retreated, fallen back to his stool and beer and is standing there, looking at nothing, square shoulders round, defeated. The young woman in the green dress sips her drink, nonplussed, eyes straight ahead again. Jack considers his opening gambit.

Serendipitously, Rachel, petulant and feeling ignored, takes the glass of ice water the bartender has delivered and tilts decisively off her stool; she stands directly behind Jack and pours most of it down the neck of her sundress, front and back. Water splatters onto the waxed, worn linoleum under her feet.

She's got Jack's full attention now. She's got the whole restaurant's attention. She makes a squeaking noise. The water is cold.

"The hell are you doing?!" the bartender growls, and starts to come from behind the bar, but Jack intercepts him calmly, acutely aware that the woman in the green dress must be watching all this, too.

"I'm sorry. She's with me," Jack says, about Rachel. "It's okay. She's my sister." He takes the towel off the bartender's shoulder, tosses it at the girl's feet and starts to mop up the ice water. "She's got—issues," Jack is ad-libbing, and he says this loud enough to be heard halfway down the bar. "Impulse control issues. I'm really sorry, man. I'll clean it up." The old ladies in the booth are buying it, their faces showing sympathy and relief (that Rachel isn't their problem). The bartender knows it's bullshit, but seems relatively disarmed by Jack's complete commitment to the role. The jarheads never look up from their plates, just want to eat before the shrimp gets cold; their dates look like they will probably believe anything.

"Are you hungry?" Jack asks Rachel, for the benefit of his intended audience just down the bar, but she's on his blind side and Jack can't tell if the woman in the green dress is even paying attention anymore.

"A little," Rachel says, going with the performance.

Jack flags the waitress, who's hurrying past with empty shrimp plates. "My sister wants to order some dinner," he says. "Can you put it on my tab?"

"You like shrimp, hon?" the waitress asks absently.

Rachel shivers, cold, her dark eyes never leaving Jack. "Deuteronomy 10: 'And whatsoever hath not fins and scales ye may not eat; it is unclean unto you.'"

"'Scuse me?"

"It's against my religion."

"Shrimp?"

"Yes, ma'am."

"And your religion is—?"

"No shrimp."

The woman in the green dress laughs out loud. The waitress shoots a slightly wounded look at her, and lets it slide contemptuously across Jack and Rachel before retreating into the kitchen. "Why'nt you look at a menu, I'll be back."

Jack nods at Rachel. "Have a seat. Sis."

Rachel's mouth is an ineluctable straight line. "Okay. Bro."

He gestures to a booth. She picks up her backpack and crosses to a banquette, where she flops down to wait, wet, staring grimly back at him. No one else in the restaurant meets her wandering gaze.

"You coming?" she says, innocently. He pretends he doesn't hear her.

Barely another moment passes before the pretty young woman stands up, smoothes her green dress, takes her glass and her shoe and limps, one shoe on, one shoe off, down the length of the bar to sit next to Jack. She still hasn't looked at him.

The marine sergeant drains his beer.

"I've seen some elaborate flirting in my time," the woman says, "but that was positively Baroque."

Jack smiles at her. "I don't know what you're talking about."

The woman in the green dress puts her shoe between herself and Jack. "I noticed you earlier. Out by the pool, under the tree. L.A., no?" Now she looks at him.

"Yes." But Jack feels the need to qualify it, "Santa Barbara, originally. I'm Jack Baylor."

"Mona Malloy. Nice to meet you, Jack."

The waitress returns from the kitchen with an order pad and crosses to the booth where Rachel is fiddling with her cell phone. The bartender asks Jack if he'd like some more coffee. Jack nods and notices, back down the bar, two bills left alone on the counter where the marine had been sitting. He is already gone, the door swinging shut behind him.

Game, set, match.

"That girl's not really your sister, is she?"

They both look at Rachel, who raises her phone and takes their picture.

"No, she's not," Jack admits, grinning winningly, he thinks, and then, before he can stop himself, asks, "The jarhead give you any trouble, Mona?"

Mona's eyes flash amusement. "Why? Were you gonna come to my defense, too?"

Fuck! Jack thinks. "If it came to that," he says, trying to salvage his play. Jesus. Shut up.

"You ever fought a marine, Jack? Even a fat, drunk one?"

Jack has still never swung, in anger or in fear, at anyone in his life. There was the one time, with Tory, but that wasn't a fight, as it turned out. "I took some Hapkido."

"Is that like Kung Fu?"

"With the sticks."

"Oh."

The Hapkido lesson was a special offer at the Fat Burn Easy spa down on Oxford, in Koreatown. At the urging of Jillian, his pre-Hannah Best Friend with Benefits, Jack joined for six months when Jillian had him convinced he was starting to put on weight. Jillian, as it turned out, never joined at all.

"Like Jet Li," Mona says.

"I'm in pretty good shape. I think I could hold my own."

Mona laughs. Jack feels the playing field tilting away from him. If he were actually standing on it, he'd be tumbling downslope, away from her, like a cartoon character. This is not going the way he needs it to.

"Pretty good shape? You look like you're in terrific shape. Mr. Ripply Abs, Bowflex, Buns of Steel." She leans into him, casual, her shoulder almost touching his, "But, see, fact of the matter is that old leatherneck, Sergeant Symes? He did three tours in Kandahar, blew out his back, got a medal and a medical discharge, and lives out in a desert double-wide, and all day long he's ex officio over at the Marine Corps Air Ground Combat Center, training young warriors and thinking about nothing but fighting and killing and getting laid, Jack. In that order. So if he decided to bother me, and you decided to come to my defense, it would probably be a very brief and unpleasant thing. And I'd probably have to step in and save you." Mona finishes her drink, one big swallow. "Which wouldn't play at all, would it?"

The middle-aged gals are leaving, tipsy, calming their weepy red-eyed friend, the one who bought the last round and nearly did a face-plant; their cosmetic laminate crinkling and those slurry, collagen smiles, sneakers shuffling across the tile floor, thanking the bartender, brushing limp, sweat-heavy bangs of their sagging perms off their faces. In her booth, Rachel pokes at a vegetarian omelet, sleepy, and tries to text something into the void. No battery. Jack shifts uneasily, figuring Mona's about to tell him to take a hike. He can't read her. Everything's gone flat. Mona stares at him until he feels about two inches tall.

Then she looks away, into her empty glass. The sadness in her smile.

"I guess you won't want me to get you another one of those?" he says softly.

Mona turns her head profile, and looks at Jack curiously out of the sides of her eyes. As if he's suddenly come into focus.

"No," she agrees, "no. Not if you won't stay until I finish it."

Half a cigarette, balanced ash-up on the edge of a bed stand, glows.

Making a suction sound as it comes off his foot, taking the sock with it, Jack's antique cowboy boot clunks loudly to the floor and flops on its side. The second boot gives up without a protest. Mona drops it, then pulls off the remaining sock with her fingertips, nose wrinkling.

"Larry Mahan," she says.

"Huh?"

Jack lies stomach-up on the bed, takes another drag on his cigarette. He's where he wants to be, and yet didn't get here in any of the usual ways. Tilt-a-Whirl, he thinks. I'm riding the ride. Mona rocks her hips back, straddles his legs, facing his feet.

"Your boots. Those are Larry Mahan boots. He was World Champion All-Around Cowboy for a few years running, back when bull riders wore Stetsons instead of helmets and the clowns were all drunks. Larry Mahan had a whole line of clothing named after him, hat to boots." Mona crawls up the bed and flattens herself against Jack's chest. "I recognize the boots by the smell."

"I thought that was just my feet."

"Nope." The straps of her faded gumball-pink brassiere have dug softly into her shoulders and back. Her pale skin shows crease marks from her clothes. Jack runs his hand along her side, up under the lace and silk of her underwear. "Everybody's feet smell the same in Larry Mahan boots," she says, shivering.

"A voice of experience."

"Lots of guys want to be World Champion Cowboys, Jack."

He traces a small tattoo on her hip: outline of a heart, thin lines blue as a vein, with the faded red promise "Always Faithful" scrawled through it on a curled banner, in script.

"The helmets have ruined it," she adds.

Her lips are dry. They skate across his neck, and down his breastbone, and over the slight rise of his stomach. Hair dusts his hipbones. Her slender hands slip under him, cool, and gentle. He feels everything and nothing. She moves slightly, adjusting her body. Small, tight breasts settle on his thighs. He strokes her neck.

There is, in the aching quiet, the dry trill of heat-dazed crickets in the vacant field behind the motel. There is the dry trill of crickets in the bush muhly and the desert needle. There is the dry trill of crickets and the promise of another day.

two

∎

Square-shouldered, blue-skinned, box-bellied Marine Sergeant John Symes sits, hunched, in a lawn chair beside the pool, staring intently up at the second-floor doors of the Rancho Del Dorotea motel. Two-oh-one through two-sixteen. Every door the same sun-blanched yellow. Between his teeth, he's expertly cracking the pistachio nuts he picks singly from the bag cradled in one fat fist.

Opposite him, in the shadow of the lone palm on the far side of the pool, Rachel is curled up on a chaise, her Hello Kitty backpack proving to be a lumpish pillow.

Probably a runaway, Symes thinks. Somebody should call somebody. Maybe there's a picture, maybe there's an Amber Alert, maybe there's a parent waiting and worrying in a crappy walk-up Riverside duplex from which the little twist fled. Maybe there's an asshole who beats her or molests her or allows the same while cooking strawberry-flavored meth in the garage. In his multiple tours of the Cradle of Civilization, Symes has seen too much to believe that insinuating himself into the landscape of other people can lead to anything other than chaos. It wasn't heroic, but most of the heroes Symes has known are either dead and buried, or prowling the streets in a permanent state of unravel.

It's just how things work.

Which is why, on balance, Symes knows he should be home sleeping instead of out here spitting husks into the darkness. "Heroes," Symes' friend Corporal Evan "Fast-Pass" Mulvey observed, not very long before they picked up the pieces of him from a roadside ditch in Helmand Province, "are just cowards with balls."

Jaw set, stubborn, angular, only Symes' sad brown eyes betray the feelings that skitter through his fretful guts as he holds vigil.

three

■

Near the rutted cliffs of Santa Monica, on a quiet stretch of the single-digit streets, a clean, white Thunderbird is double-parked in front of a six-plex. The car's vanity plate reads: TORY G.

In an upstairs apartment, Tory Geller stands contemplating the familiar, cluttered front room, entry door open behind him. An angry car horn blares outside in the darkness, protest of a passing motorist forced to swerve past the T-bird.

Tory disappears down the unlit hallway.

In his wake lies the detritus of Jack Baylor's existence: clothing, running shoes, pile of dog-eared scripts, books in stacks against the wall, outdated PC, flat-screen television, TiVo, tower of DVDs and CDs, flattened basketball, long-shaft putter out and leaning against the unmade sofa bed, posters from a few indie movies, a stained and cracked fiberglass surfboard, and an inflatable pterodactyl hanging from the ceiling.

Tory comes back holding a fat, brown-and-black Tonganese with a nervously twitching tail.

"Where'd he go, Murphy? Where's handsome?"

A phone machine sits atop a stack of old phone books on a table in the corner. On its face is balanced a small yellow Post-it pad, and on this is scrawled a number and the words *Rancho Del Dorotea*.

Murphy the cat purrs recklessly.

The lids of Tory Geller's eyes sink to half-mast, and he digs in his pocket for the golf tee he found under the bed in Montecito, to return it to the collection of tees and ball markers in the Davy Crockett water glass beside the answering machine.

four

■

A red neon sign pulses: VACANCY. A girl in a sundress sleeps, and dreams she is sleeping. An empty lawn chair waits on the edge of a desert motel pool, pale red pistachio shells neatly scattered on the ground around and under it like tea leaves waiting to be read.

five

■

There is the bleed of far-flung televisions, and that specific TV blue that ghosts the walls flutters across the queen-sized beds and half-shadowed faces above machine-quilted polyester bedspreads; a dream shared, or dreams, overlapping, felt truly but later forgotten, like a dog-eared copy of the CliffsNotes on *Jack's Life Until Now*. His thoughts grind, unruly. Stop, he tells himself. Just stop. One of his hands is interlocked with hers, and in that Fuzzy Warm Aftermath it would be hard for him to say where his body ends and Mona's begins. There is her hair across the side of his face. There is the soft compression of her happily worn-out breathing.

"Oh. My. Goodness."

Jack's feet have socks on them, Mona's are wagging, double-time. Their hands untangle. Bedsprings creak.

"Oh, hey, whoa, don't, no no no no, shit, don't, don't drop that on the carpet, okay?" Mona props herself up on one arm, peering in at Jack through the open bathroom doorway as he stands drilling urine into the backwater of the toilet bowl. "They leave these spots that're all hell to clean," she explains.

"You have some experience in that area, too?" Jack shakes and returns.

"I work here." She lets his surprise register, while Jack, being the actor, tries unsuccessfully to conceal it. "Yeah. I bet you had me figured for some lonely local who goes to the Roundup Room hoping romance will make a road stop."

At the foot of the bed, Jack stands, looking down at her. That *is* pretty much what he had figured.

Mona gropes for Jack's cigarettes, which she finds practically crushed underneath her. "Also, I live here. Room one-twenty-four, on the end." She looks up at him. "My mom owns this place."

Jack's mind empties. Any plans he had of choreographing the rest of this weekend sift through his fingers.

"Your mom?"

Mona taps out a deformed cigarette. "Want to meet her? See what I'm going to look like in about thirty years?"

Jack fumbles the lighter from the bed stand onto the bed. Why would she say that? Mona fishes for it in the swirl of sheets, lights her own cigarette. She's still smiling, and Jack is unnerved.

"You're not such a nice guy, are you, Jack?"

"I could be."

"Ah."

"Look, Mona—"

"Relax. Mom's gone to La Costa for the week, to troll for guys who run hedge funds and pop Viagra like breath mints." Mona touches him lightly, on the arm. "Don't wig out on me, Jack. I'm a grown woman. Or a big girl, to borrow your quaint worldview. Either way? I do what I want." She puffs on the cigarette somewhat awkwardly, like someone who never really learned, then puts it between Jack's lips, glancing at the silver lighter, where there's an engraved inscription that reads simply: MAD ABOUT THE BOY. Mona frowns at it.

"I'm fine," Jack says dryly.

"Fine." She looks up at him.

"Yes."

"I just thought I should tell you. I didn't have to."

"Tell me what?"

"About Mom."

"No. You didn't." Jack's wondering why she did tell him, now, what it implies if it implies anything, mistrusting any of the well-honed instincts that have guided him to this moment. He wants to run, and yet he wants to stay, for once, to find out why he would want to run.

"You don't have a sister, do you? I mean, a real one."

"No." She waits. He tries to think of something else to offer her in the way of personal detail. "I was an only child."

"Me, too."

"I don't have kids, I'm not married."

"Really? No kidding."

An uncertain smile crawls across Jack's features. Was that sarcasm? He's off the map of his flat world. Over the edge, into unknown territories where medieval cartographers wrote: *Here be dragons.* "What?" he says defensively. "You don't think I could be married, or have kids?"

"Oh, you could definitely have kids, given the, well, enthusiasm and determination you apply to the task. And I bet there's a landfill of broken hearts who hoped or mistakenly believed you might want to marry them."

"That's harsh."

"Harsh nothing. Statement of fact. Want to dance?"

"What?"

"Dance."

"I can't."

"Bullshit."

"You think I'm an asshole, but you still want to dance with me?"

"I know. However, (a): I didn't say you were an asshole, you did, and (b): I just hooked up with you, Jack, and I don't fuck assholes—but, since you brought it up, okay, well, it has been my experience that assholes can be great dancers."

"I don't—"

"C'mon."

Jack says stubbornly, "I can't dance. I'm sorry." He adds, somewhat more artificially: "I can't dance, I doubt there's a God, and I don't make decisions without knowing what all the options are."

Mona rolls her eyes. She's already off the bed, and pulling Jack's shirt over her head and throwing his jeans at him, offering only, "That is so weak."

The Roundup Room is dark. Chairs on the tables, stools up on the bar. Mona unlocks the door and pulls Jack inside. He has no shirt, because Mona's wearing it, no shoes because she wouldn't let him take the time to put on his boots. Mona's small body barely curves the cotton of Jack's shirt as she goes behind the bar to light a couple of votive candles and turn on the stereo. Samba music. The snap of the *surdo*, the *pandeiro* shivers its reply.

"My granddad built this place in 1951 for a woman who was not his wife."

"Dorotea?"

Mona pours reposado into shot glasses. "Dorotea Elana Maria Bustos Pacheco, a Peruvian nightclub singer my granddad met in Denver. He was already married then—I think my mom was about two or three—but he was an accountant for a resort chain and they used to send him out to do the country club audits. Señorita Pacheco was playing the Blue Spruce Room at Cherry Hills Country Club. She was one of those big-boned women with the little tiny waists. There's some pictures of her over the motel office—dark hair, dark eyes, big wide mackerel mouth smeared with dark, wicked-witch lipstick.

"Well, Granddad had never experienced oral sex of any kind, and she, by all accounts, could suck-start a Harley, and so before you could say *adios*, he and 'Tea were headed west to California in his berry-red Buick ragtop. It broke down in Victorville, crawled here and died. They built this motel so she'd have someplace to sing. Between blow jobs. Built it with money he'd neatly disappeared from his employer's development fund."

"They come after him?"

"Never went after him. Or after my grandmother, who, for no apparent reason, subsequently became a Mormon. I think Granddad Malloy knew how hard the resort chain's books were cooked, since he'd done a lot of the culinary heavy lifting, so they just wrote down the loss and left him alone.

"My mom ran away from home when she was fifteen and hitchhiked out here to Two-nine Palms to be with her dad.

"Then 'Tea got pregnant by Granddad's best friend Norbert Willams, and then she died in childbirth—she was so small through the middle and the baby got itself hung up in there— subsequently Granddad wigged out. He started smoking reefer and hanging with would-be gold prospectors and land speculators and professional lowlifes in Yucca Valley."

Mona comes out from behind the bar. Hands Jack a shot glass. "He either got killed in a head-on collision outside of Blythe or ran off to San Francisco, my mom is kind of unclear about it. But, hey, she's been running this place by herself since she was twenty"—Mona raises her shot glass—"survived me and the desert and has no regrets."

They drink. Then Mona takes his glass, and puts it with hers, side-by-side, on the bar.

"I think the trouble with choices, Jack, is there's too many of them. You can't ever know them all."

"That's why I never make decisions," Jack says.

"You do. You will." Mona moves close to him, kisses him hard. "Mad about the boy."

"Yes." Jack starts to put his arms around her, but she catches them, pulls him into position and starts to move her hips. "Wait—"

"Dancing is about trust."

"Yeah, well, and maybe rhythm, which I don't have."

"Come on."

"I'm serious, Mona. I can't dance."

"You have to, Jack. Sooner or later." She stares into his eyes. He knows she can see the difference. The grey one, with its overcast cornea and fixed pupil, looks but doesn't see. Jack can feel her question even if she doesn't ask it, and for a moment they are only movement. "Nice guys dance," Mona says finally.

Jack is awful, no matter how hard he concentrates. His feet never find the rhythm. Mona, however, doesn't appear to care.

Later, Jack sits cross-legged on the bed back in his motel room, quartering a lime with a carving knife borrowed from the Roundup Room bar. The half-empty bottle of tequila waits on the bed stand, with more whole limes in a bowl, and a saltshaker alongside Jack's signature cigarette, smoldering, vertical, end up.

Mona flicks Jack's lighter, and the flame licks out. Extinguishes it with the cap. Flicks it on again. Extinguishes it.

"You've lived out here how long?"

"All my life, except for a few intermissions. Scout camp in Ensenada. Disney World. And this other thing that happened." Mona sits up. Flick, flick, flick.

Jack wonders: other thing?

"I understand the desert," she says finally. "All the emptiness."

Jack puts the knife on the bed stand, gives Mona a wedge of lime and the bottle. "Where's your dad?"

"Mom claims he's a Hollywood movie star who came out here and broke her heart. She swears she only slept with him twice." Mona stares at him, swigs tequila, sucks on the lime, salts her tongue. "And she made it a cautionary tale, you know, about sex and pregnancy. Was that the right order?"

"Yes. Sex, then pregnancy."

"No, with the limes and—"

"To be truthful, I don't think there is a right order." Jack tosses tequila, jams his lime wedge against his teeth and eschews the salt. The liquor kicks, doesn't go down right, burns hot in his chest.

"I personally think Dad was a fall-down drunken gyrene grunt Mom used as a sperm donor because she was thirty-six and figured she'd never get the chance again."

Jack swallows hard a second time, his eyes watering as Mona crawls back on top of him. She's got the lighter. "Somebody give you this?"

"Yeah."

"Wife?"

"Old girlfriend."

"How old?"

He pictures Hannah, only hours ago, in her snowy swirl of down. "History." It seems so long ago. Jillian, lithe and elusive. Others (so many?) blur together like photos in a high school annual, heads cocked, smiles frozen, eyes inert. Done and gone.

"Mad. About the boy."

Now Mona waits. Jack doesn't want to talk about it anymore. "It's a line from a movie."

Mona frowns. "I don't mean this as criticism, or being judgmental, or anything," she says, "but it sounds gay."

"*Sunset Boulevard.*"

"What?"

"*Sunset Boulevard.* Gloria Swanson, William Holden?" Mona's face is expressionless. "You know it?"

"No."

"You've never seen *Sunset Boulevard*?"

"No."

"Famous movie."

"If you *were* gay, it'd be okay with me, just a little, well, confusing."

"And then it was a musical."

"Okay. Yeah, guess I missed it."

For some reason Jack thinks: good.

"I'm not that interested in movies."

"Oh."

"Or musicals. I'm more a television gal." She adds, "You do have a kind of metrosexual thing going on, though."

"What are you talking about?"

"Nothing. Nothing."

An awkward moment passes. Mona puts the lighter on the bed stand. Takes the cigarette from vertical, taps the ashes into the lime bowl, and takes a deep, last drag. "So why'd you come out here, Jack? You come all the way out here to fuck me and break my heart?"

"No."

"What do you do? Do I even want to know? Let me guess. Not management, Hughes Aircraft or something, buying parts. No. You're way, way too sketchy for the real world." She stares at him. "Something creative. Art? No, art requires commitment. Web design or something."

"Not even close." Jack indulges himself with what he believes to be a suitable pause before he says, "I am an actor."

"No way." Mona giggles.

Jack shrugs. "Way."

"No."

"Way."

"Get out. What have you been in?"

"Nothing. Well, a lot of nothing. TV. I'm the guy who plays the parts you don't remember. *Wildwood,* couple times."

"What?"

"*Wildwood.*"

"I loved that show. Who were you?"

"I thought you didn't like—"

"I love television."

"It's not—"

"—I should know who you—"

"—Michael's shy and sensitive second cousin. Chastity has erotic dreams about me. Then finds out I'm gay. Or what passes for gay in 1799."

"Oh. A pattern developing."

"It was a role. It was a part I played."

"I don't remember a cousin."

"Five scenes. Two episodes. Twenty-eight lines."

"Terry?"

"Tom."

"I'm not wrong, though—actor? In touch with your feminine side? Emotional, overcompensating on the machismo even, but—"

"Can we talk about something else?"

Mona's eyes shine. "Do Tom for me."

"No."

"Just one line."

"No."

"You can't remember one line?"

"It's been awhile."

"You can too. I'll bet you remember every line."

It's weird, but Jack does.

"Or make one up." He won't do it. Mona seems genuinely disappointed. Jack wets his finger with his tongue, uses it to kill the cigarette. Carefully, he tries to replace it end-up on the nightstand, but misjudges the distance and it falls onto the floor and neither Jack nor Mona sees it go.

"Your turn," Jack says. "If you're so paranoid about it, why did you let me come out here and fuck you?"

"Low self-esteem?"

"Seriously."

"Seriously?" She makes a thinking face. "Seriously. Well, I'm not all that complicated, Jack. You're cute, you're funny, you've got a great ass. I like your smile, your phony, cocksure, manly man routine winds my clock, I can't explain it." She puts her hand on his face, gently. Her unapologetic vulnerability takes his breath away, but not like the first time he saw her, because now he knows her. And now it troubles him. "I don't know, could be the best answer. What can I say? I just did. I just wanted to and I did."

"And your heart?"

"Is the dumb guy. Lousy memory, always the optimist."

Jack doesn't know what to say next.

"It doesn't happen all that often," Mona adds softly.

"I come out here to get away from the city," Jack tells her, to break the silence. "All the artificial stuff that goes on back there."

"As opposed to . . . here?"

"You know."

"No. Our In-and-Out is more 'real' than yours? Our mini-malls have some essential truth you can't find back in L.A.? Explain this to me."

"It's just, it's like you can get so caught up in it. The spin, the swirl, you start swirling, too," Jack hears himself saying. "I'm not a movie star, I'm not part of the scene. I do what I do and go home, like anybody else. Except, in L.A., you can't escape it."

"Caught up in . . . the artificial stuff."

"Yes."

"Like, Astroturf and plastic flowers and—"

Jack is determined to make his point. "No, like, plastic surgery, okay? Fake tits, surgical smiles, the culture of celebrity, martinis at the Skybar. Designer dogs."

"Oh no, you're one of those guys who says *tits*."

"What?"

Mona is laughing, delighted. "And? Finish your thought."

Jack's mind double clutches. And?

Coyotes cackle crazily in the distant creosote flats and Jack tries one more time, stubborn, deadpan. "I come out here to look at the desert and, I know, I know, okay, it sounds stupid, but I come out here and get in touch with myself. What's real, what's not. What's important." He can't finish because Mona's laughing. "Okay."

"I'm sorry." She can't stop laughing, though. "I'm sorry. The coyotes."

"No it's not."

"No it's not, but—"

"You think I'm full of shit?"

"I don't." Mona's tone is sweet and caring and delighted. "No. It's. Well, maybe a little. Yes. Yes I do. But then no, not totally."

"I am. I'm full of shit."

She touches him. "Don't say that. You're not," she says, eyes smiling, "but I bet, sometimes? You tell people what you think they want you to say, or maybe just what you think sounds like it might be true, and maybe that works with most people but not me, for a whole variety of reasons you don't need to know, Jack."

"That sounds like someone who's full of shit."

"It does, doesn't it?"

The silence is Jack's.

"I'm sorry. Truly. It doesn't matter. I'm just so happy. You can see that, can't you? I don't know why, and I don't know why I started to laugh, something about you talking and the coyotes barking was funny, I laughed, and I couldn't stop. I don't know why."

Jack's not angry. "But you think I'm sort of full of shit."

"No." Mona kisses him, giggling again. "Yes. No"—her arms around him—"no I don't. Eventually I won't." She fills his arms, warm, alive, and everything, and Jack is happy and won't start worrying what she means by *eventually* until much later.

six

■

A hot wind blows through the Joshua tree forest. Flags stir on blistered metal poles, swamp coolers kick in, dust devils whirl down vacant streets, but the trees are unmoved.

The same hot wind slips through the curtains of Jack's room, and across the bed where he lies motionless, sleeping, sweating.

"Housekeeping!"

Jack opens his eyes to the day, there's banging at the door, and then the rattle of a key in the lock.

"Jesus—wait a sec—" He scrambles for his jeans at the foot of the bed, but the door opens before he can pull them on. In strides Mona, pushing the housekeeping cart. T-shirt, baggy shorts, her hair pulled back and tied with a scarf; she looks great, ten years younger and happier than when she walked into his life and the Roundup Room last night.

"I'm sorry, should I come back later?" She closes the door behind her, with no intention of leaving.

"Um—"

"Hi."

Jack's jeans are jammed around his knees. He hauls them up. Mona watches, tickled by his modesty. "You should've got me up when you left," he says.

"I left at five-thirty AM, Mr. Grouchy. We would've needed jumper cables and a winch. Breakfast?"

Sure enough, there are coffee and muffins on a tray atop the housekeeping cart. Mona puts the tray on the nightstand, sweeps the bar knife into the drawer with the limes, and throws the empty tequila bottle into a plastic garbage bag that hangs from her cart. "Compliments of the management."

Jack, wolfing a muffin down his dry throat, can't find a voice.

"Don't say anything you're gonna regret."

"What kind of muffin is this?"

"Dingleberry."

He frowns, chewing. He's pretty sure there is no such thing.

"Gonna go out and stare at the desert today?"

"You're making fun of me."

"No. Not yet."

"Funny. Yeah, okay, yeah, I want to drive into the national park and see the cholla gardens."

Mona starts to pull the sheets off the bed, then stops. "Shit, Jack! I told you not to drop these on the carpet! Shit! Yuck!" She kneels down to pick up a lumpish prophylactic between two fingers and quickly, distastefully, drops it into the black plastic trash bag on the side of her cart, after which she unhappily looks under the bed for more.

Jack wonders, deadpan: "Now how did that get there?"

Unamused, Mona sprays the rug with carpet cleaner, and scrubs hard at it with a brush. "I hate this part."

"I'm sorry. I forgot."

Jack gets down next to her, gently takes the brush away, and starts working. Mona rocks back on her heels and watches him.

"The other day it occurred to me. All day I pick up the little bits and pieces that break off people's lives. That's what I do. The skin cells that slough off in bed, in the tub, in the sink, on the sofa. Toenails. Hair. Pubic hair. Eyelashes. Saliva, bodily fluids."

Jack cuts a grossed-out do-I-need-to-know-that glance at her, stops scrubbing carpet, and frowns at the spot. "I think that got it."

"And yet. If I could put them all together, I wonder, I wonder if I'd have even one whole complete life."

Jack looks at her again, unsure where this will go.

"Wouldn't that be weird?" Mona smiles. "On the plus side, maybe I wouldn't have to keep hooking up with guys like you." Jack says nothing, just looks at her with a calm he hasn't felt before.

"What."

"You're prettier than I remember."

Jack leans forward to kiss her, but Mona pushes him away. "Shut up. Hey. Behave. Don't look at me like that. Now listen, I want to show you something later. After you go see the cacti."

"Show me what?"

"If I tell you, it won't be a surprise."

"I don't like surprises."

"Tough."

Mona sticks her tongue out at him and starts to stand up, but Jack tackles her back onto the carpet. "No. Jack, come on, I'm working—" She laughs. He tugs her shirttail out of her shorts. "Oh, Jesus, take a cold shower, will you—come on, no, no, oh no, oh, I've gotta have these rooms cleaned by eleven. Jack—" She relaxes, though. "—Oh Jack—" Mona stops struggling. Jack pins her down, unbuttons her shorts, and starts to roll them off, and Mona is helping him, arching her hips. "Now I'm going to be all sweaty again."

Rachel and her Hello Kitty backpack don't get a second glance as she wanders down the sidewalk of the main street. There are knots in her hair, and slivers of cracked patio furniture vinyl stuck to her rumpled sundress, but, still, as far as anyone can tell, she's got to be from a family of tourists, their RV parked just around the corner, the rest of the brood's having breakfast and she's walking back to get something from the vehicle.

Huge, painted eyes behind dark-rimmed glasses watch her, vigilant, distrustful, from a long mural that spans the wall across the street. And, sure enough, she stops at the door, not of the family RV, but of a station wagon with a luggage shell strapped on top like a huge suppository, and she tugs on the handle as if expecting it to open. Locked. Undaunted, she moves to the next car, all casual, as if she hadn't tried the door of the last one. Locked. And the next. Locked. And the next. Finally finding the door to a clean white T-bird unlocked, she quickly slips inside and disappears into the cool shadows behind a sun-blanched windshield.

The T-bird has vanity plates: TORY G.

Across the street, Tory Geller is inside the front office of the Motel Del Dorotea, talking pleasantly to the day clerk, a sad young man who keeps self-consciously touching a swollen pimple on his neck.

Tory doesn't see Jack come out of his room or descend the metal stairs. Jack doesn't see Tory. At his car, Jack unlocks the door with an actual key—there's no remote—adjusts his sunglasses, runs his hand through wet hair, then gets in and backs up and drives around the pool and out the rear exit, which Tory, his old friend, also cannot see.

After a moment, Tory comes out of the office and looks up toward the second floor, and Jack's room.

In the T-bird, Rachel is methodically rooting through the car for booty. She reaches under the seat and finds a gun-shop bag containing a brand-new Bersa Thunder 380 D.A. concealed-carry pistol complete with a Houston holster and a box of Federal 90-grain JHP bullets. The pistol is black and mean, and the receipt is still in the bag.

At first she thinks it must be a toy, but the weight of it scares her. Rachel nervously stuffs the gun and bag back where she found them, pops open the glove compartment, and empties it of its contents, putting the gun out of her mind. First, there is a half-used tube of dark pink lipstick, which she tries on her mouth. It's not bad. She ignores the stash of folded cash money (she's not a thief), the registration pink slip, the pencils (but remembers a math test coming up on Friday), folded Kleenex, finally finding what she's come for, what she instinctively knows will be in every glove compartment of every American car, wedged way in back: three tinfoil packets of Wet'n Dry towelettes.

As he comes up the motel stairs, Tory pauses politely to let the maid (MONA on her name tag) go past with her housekeeping cart. He smells her as she passes, notices the slender curve of her leg, the dampness on her upper lip, the steady cast of her eyes. She opens the door of a room and disappears inside. Nice.

Tory walks down to Jack's room, knocks on the door, and waits. No one answers. There is the muffled sound of the maid's vacuum cleaner starting up in the next room, and the whir of the pool pump, and a waterfall of faraway highway traffic, and the hiss of the wind, and the pounding of his pulse against his eardrums, which will not stop.

Tory turns and looks darkly out east across the languorous, sun-struck jumble of downtown Twentynine Palms. He's got time.

Bathing with the three towelettes, Rachel is startled by a sharp slap on the T-bird window and it causes her to freeze, mid-wash. She looks up, scared, into the guileless grey eyes of a lean sheriff's deputy named Ng.

Ten miles down the two-lane blacktop that winds through the broken round-rock terrain of Joshua Tree National Park like the stroke of a magic marker on a blistered cardboard, there is a big horseshoe bend and a turnoff where visitors can leave their cars and walk through the cholla gardens. Jack pulls off to park his Buick beside an old canary yellow Mercedes station wagon nosed into the thorny bushes. Not far away, three middle-aged women in relaxed-fit jeans are bent over examining the flora, looking to Jack very much like alien pods planted optimistically in the bleak terra cotta. They straighten up, and Jack immediately recognizes the margarita gals from the Roundup Room, Paula and her friends.

After a short conference, the tallest, Emma, comes walking out to Jack's car. She's got a handful of cactus flowers and picks her way carefully along the path. "Excuse me." Jack rises, leans over his car door like it's a fence. Emma takes in Jack's faded denim shirt, jeans, and World Champion Cowboy boots, and he realizes that she doesn't remember him. "Can you tell us something about the cholla? Where the name comes from, I mean."

"Maybe he's not a ranger," warns the oldest one, Florence, squinting and pushing a wisp of clean silver hair back up with its friends. Paula, the one Jack caught and kept upright, is just frowning at him, hands set on bony hips.

"It's a Spanish name, ma'am." Jack uses his best Park Ranger voice. "Literally, it means skull or head."

"He says it means skull," Emma calls back to her friends.

"The Indians named it. There's one cholla for every individual in each of the Indian nations. Native Americans believed that the desert, which they called *Mohave*, was the entrance to hell and that the cholla stayed here to keep evil spirits from going back to haunt the tribe, and to prevent good spirits from becoming lost in the desert and accidentally winding up in hell." The words are just cartwheeling out.

"Is the flesh edible?"

Paula makes a derisive, hungover sound.

"The Indians thought eating the flesh of the cholla would cause you to take on the evil spirit trapped inside," Jack explains, as if patiently. "In fact, it's incredibly poisonous. Convulsions, then death." Florence and Emma have worried frowns, but Paula is slowly walking back to the car, looking tired and in pain.

"Bullshit," she barks out. "He's the one from the saloon last night, kept me from falling on my butt." She looks over at Jack. "With little Mona, right? You don't work for the park service."

Emma shakes her head. "If he doesn't work for the park service, how does he know so much about cholla?"

Jack smiles. "She's right. I'm a fraud. I'm a chollologist from Fresno. We're trying to develop a hybrid for the home gardener."

"He's yanking our chain again," Paula gripes to her friends. "You're yanking our chain," she tells Jack. She gets into the car, slams the door. The other women are walking back to join her. "It's not a fair fight," Paula is yelling from inside the car, muffled. "I got an asshat of a hangover."

"A poisonous plant for the home?" Emma wonders.

"Or office. Adds to the exotic appeal," Jack says.

In the station wagon, Paula leans on the horn. It echoes, brittle, rattles around the rocks.

"Paula wants to go to Palm Springs. We want to drive through the park and see more flowers," Florence explains.

"We're the majority," Emma adds. Paula keeps honking. "All right! All right!" Emma ducks into the car, behind the wheel, and cranks the starter until it grinds.

"Give it gas!" Paula yells.

Florence pats Jack on the shoulder as she goes past him. "You seem like a nice man. Don't hurt our Mona, 'kay? We know her mother."

"Don't worry about it," Jack says.

"We are leaving!"

"Paula shouldn't drink tequila," Florence observes. More irritated honking from the car. Emma and Paula fall into an argument they've clearly had before. "Mona's had a string of bad luck with men," she adds. Florence opens her door. "Take her away from here. Take her back to Fresno with you. Or wherever. It's too hot here." She gets in the car, slams the door shut.

Emma rolls down the window. "You like kids? She's got a couple of real cuties, Mona does."

"Shut up, Emma," Paula says.

"I'm just saying."

"He could give a shit," Paula says.

Jack's smile is frozen on his face as they drive away.

* * *

Rachel was determined not to tell them anything after the deputy caught her looking through the glove box of the car, but they took her phone away, and got everything they needed from the SIM card. Name, address, the phone number of her parents, her calling plan, the number of minutes she used, text messages from her friends, the video of Kenny trying to learn how to ollie. Sitting on a hard chair in the police station, she regrets not hiding it under the seat of the T-bird. Or dropping it accidentally into a storm drain as she walked to the patrol car, which smelled like vomit and cologne and air fresheners, and had doors without handles just like on TV; they were trying to scare her with their solemn, tough faces and terse instructions, like high school gym teachers, or assistant principals, two species Rachel had long ago tamed. But the cell phone meant they would summon her parents, and that, as they say, would be that.

At least the discovery of her phone rescued her from the usual dog-and-pony show that the Adults in Authority, in her admittedly limited experience, loved to throw at wayward youth in a lame and awkward attempt to persuade them that the path of juvenile delinquency was a dead end.

To which Rachel could only respond: duh.

Across the empty squad room she watches Ng talk, low, calm, professional, on the desk phone. She can't read his lips, but his expression tells her that her mother is, for once, at home. No doubt horrified. And so disappointed. Disappointment is where her mother lives these days. In a minute, the cop will put the receiver down, hitch up his pants, walk over to where Rachel is sitting, and let her know that her parents are on their way.

She will not cry. She won't react.

Consequentially, Ng will probably put her into a holding cell in back for a while, as long as there are no other criminals in residence, maybe he even prearranged it with her mom, "to teach her a lesson," scared straight, shock and awe, or—what'd they call it?

Tough love.

Sure.

As if, Rachel muses, there is any other kind.

The first rock misses, but the next one glances off the back of Jack's head, sending a single cartoon star spinning, and the slow bite of pain. Thinking it's an accident but knowing it isn't, hoping to hear a timid "sorry!" from somewhere upslope, instead Jack sees, too late, a third rock knuckle in and drill him high on the shoulder. "Owshit!" The two little kids duck back behind a huge boulder and their giggles carry.

"Zach?! Carrie?!" Mona comes along the trail carrying their picnic. She hasn't seen the ambush. Behind the motel, a web of crisscrossing rocky paths allows guests to get a blush of desert without making the drive into the national park. There are some picnic tables and mismatched patio furniture, a prefab gazebo thatched with the dead limbs of a bougainvillea somebody planted years ago, watered for a while, then evidently abandoned to the heat.

"If you go, oh, about a mile on up this trail there's a sort of inspiration point where you can look back across the valley," Mona is telling Jack, "and sometimes even see the smoke from field exercises at Combat Town, on the marine base," she's rambling, happy. "It's where they train our guys how to deal with your various civilian situations over in the Middle East. There's a lot of shouting involved. Sometimes they set stuff on fire. For the verisimilitude and whatnot. I don't know where they find all the Arab people, we never see them around here."

Mona spreads a blanket, and as she's turned away from Jack another rock sails down and bangs him in the thigh. Fuck. The kid has an arm. Instinctively, he keeps his back to the hill.

"Zach and Carrie! Lunch!" She straightens, brushes hair out of her eyes. "Did you see where they went?"

"No." Two kids, no wedding ring. Should he have seen it coming? He let his guard down, let her over the border, and now he's struggling to reconcile the certainty of his desire with the unconditional inflexibility of his dogma. "Ow—!"

And dodging rocks.

"What?" Mona hears the stone skitter away, looks at Jack with a question he can't answer, because the rocks are, he thinks, well, deserved somehow. Invited.

"I think they're up behind that big—"

"Are they throwing rocks at you?"

A handful of pebbles rains down on them. "Stop it!" Mona cries, in a flat, hard, parental tone Jack still can't quite believe is in her range. "Stop it right now!" A cease-fire ensues, but no insurgents emerge from the rocks above them. Mona closes her eyes in embarrassment. "It's not you."

"You don't think?"

"No." She won't elaborate, and Jack doesn't want to ask. They sit on the blanket in the shade to eat their sandwiches, and the hot desert wind blows quiet and the scuffing of small shoes and whispering of high voices belies the presence of Zach and Carrie, but Mona's children remain in hiding.

"I'm sorry."

"Don't sweat it."

"They—"

"—I know."

"It's not you."

"You said that." Jack adds, candidly, "It could be me."

The tears come suddenly. Out of nowhere, a thunderstorm of sadness that catches even Mona by surprise. Sadness that bends her, shoulders caved, head down, hands twisted. Tears that splash on Jack's arms as he tries, awkwardly, to comfort her, but her body is hard, closed off. With some twisting of blanket and legs Jack manages to get her head against his chest and it feels all wrong; there's faint tenderness to it, and after what seems like too long he relents and sits back, helpless, to watch as she cries and cries and Jack can't remember when a woman's crying has ever affected him so completely. He's just starting to assess the significance of this when another rock caroms off his head. "Ow!"

Mona is up on her feet, wiping her eyes with her arm and stumbling up half-blind into the rocks to find her children. "All right, that's enough! Zachary? Do you hear me? That is enough!" She disappears, and Jack might as well be alone. There is the wind, and the heat. A lazy squeak-trill of a raven. A grasshopper's rasp.

There are voices, too, distant, angry, defiant, remorseful; a full cache of emotions that Jack can, if needed, summon on command.

This timid riot of color.

The flying constable squints, two-dimensional, tanned, somewhat adobe-brown and—oh sweet Jesus, is he smiling or grimacing?—snaggle-toothed, right out at Tory from the epic mural covering the lee side of Crossroads Christian Bookstore. It's as if the constable damn well knows what's on Tory's mind, which, for Tory, in his present state of agitation, is exceptionally disturbing. The heat from the wall makes the painted face flex and stir. Tory decides that this will be the last stop on his self-guided tour of the Twentynine Palms "Oasis of Murals," because the accumulation of images is starting to creep him out. He balls up the informational flyer and tosses it into the T-bird, to join the note from the cop named Ng, who says to call if anything is missing from the car. Nothing is, so Tory can see no need to open that door; his fortunately scant contact with law enforcement has taught him never to voluntarily engage the police, since they are more than capable of finding you when they need you.

The sun is low, burning through the polarized windows of the Joshua Tree National Park visitor center gift shop when, a little later, Tory buys four novelty postcards (two jackalopes, a giant trout, and a picture of a man neck deep in snow, captioned, "The Trouble with Short Horses in Montana"), and a tin of California rock candy. The cashier rings it up. A small group of tourists crowds a lecturing park ranger outside, in the palm-studded seminar courtyard.

"The Serrano Indians named the high desert Mar-ah. Land of little water. This Oasis of Mar-ah may have been a holy place, where medicine men claimed the water would help produce healthy boy babies, but geologically it is the upshot of water rising to the surface along the Pinto Mountain Fault. Land on the north is moving westward and land on the south is moving eastward, causing tension to build over time, explaining the periodic earthquakes we'll get, as well as the transport of water to the surface at this location from the underground aquifers that lie far beneath this barren desert."

Tory folds in with the tourists, sucking a rock candy, staring out at the small stand of parched palm trees, pathetic native grasses, and dull, round rocks that surround a tiny accident of vegetation in the rolling hardscrabble and dust. He's never understood Jack's fascination with the high desert. Hot, ugly, and desolate, it's a place you drive through, fast, to get to Laugh-lin or Vegas. Or fly over. And again he begins to resent the errand that's brought him here: Jack, Jack's fuck-up. That Jack could even unintentionally make such a full and complete claim on Tory's attention. How did *that* happen?

"It appears the Indians planted the palm trees in a specific pat-tern, perhaps relating to the whole boy-baby fertility thing. We don't know. Later, white settlers and prospectors found the oasis and named it Twentynine Palms . . ." The ranger laughs spon-taneously at this private joke. Clueless, the tourists smile, wait until he gathers himself. "Although, as far as anyone knows, there have never been more than the twenty-six palm trees you see now."

Tittering laughter from the tourists, polite but uncertain.

The voice that comes from the back is dead and sharp: "I don't get it." Heads turn toward Tory, for he has broken the polite wall that ritually separates audience from lecturer, and they take exception to it, but Tory keeps going, "I mean, hell, twenty-six palm trees, they name it Twentynine Palms? Am I a moron? Makes no sense."

"It's, I don't know, ironic, I guess."

"What?"

"Ironic. Absurdity of life," the ranger says blithely. "*Tout comprendre, c'est tout pardonner.*"

"*Ne se comprend pas.* Asshole. It doesn't make sense," Tory insists stubbornly.

"No it doesn't, it doesn't," the ranger concedes, with only the weariest hint of sarcasm. "And I can't explain it, sir."

"Well you shouldn't tell a story you can't explain."

"How's that?"

"You shouldn't tell a story you can't fucking explain."

The horrified silence of propriety completely violated.

"I'll keep that in mind, sir." A professional smile. Everything under control.

Tory is already walking away, disgusted. He figures his friend should be back at the motel by now.

In fact, Jack is on the phone, smoking, shirt off. A still, dark silhouette. The embers of the dying day cool, framed in the balcony window, sun snagged on the worn-down sawtooth horizon. On the other end of Jack's call, a phone rings and rings and rings. "Hi. This is Jillian," the voicemail answers. "I'm not here, but leave your name and number."

The door opens and Mona slips in, swallowed by the shadows when she closes the door again. Jack hears the beep of the message prompt. For a moment Jack is speechless. He looks at Mona; she puts her finger to her lips, understanding, and sits on the edge of the bed.

Barely moving, Jack presses his thumb to disconnect, hangs up the call, but begins talking as if he hasn't: "You're kidding. No, no, I have to come back for that. You're right. Absolutely." Jack wonders whether he's conning Mona or himself.

He presses the phone into his ear so the buzzing dial tone won't leak out and give him away. "Tomorrow. Okay, I will. Thanks, Paul." He racks the receiver, looks at Mona. He can make out only the outline of her face. She's intent upon her restless hands. She smoothes the patterned bedspread.

"You're going back."

"Tomorrow," Jack lies.

"Not like there's a waiting list for the room, or anything."

"That was my agent. Something came up. ADR. That's when you re-do dialogue for a scene, or . . ."

"Uh-huh." She nods at nothing. "You don't have a cell phone?"

"No."

"I would think an actor would be glued to—"

"—I'm taking a break from the cellular world, actually. My phone crapped out, and—"

"—now you're a Luddite."

"What?"

"Back to basics. People who eschew technology. Luddites."

"Eschew?"

"Yeah. Deliberately avoid using. Or abstain from."

"Okay, right. But—"

"Jack, I just wanted to apologize for today. The kids. Zach, he's—"

"There's nothing to apologize for."

"There is. And he's going to."

"It's okay, Mona. He's just a kid."

"It's not okay. It's not acceptable."

Jack stares at her. He loves her eyes, clear, steady, holding his, fierce. Mona frowns.

"What."

"Something's . . . wrong with—"

"It's blind," Jack says. "My eye. This one, it's blind. Sometimes it looks like I'm not listening, because my line of sight is just off center." Mona gets up and walks closer, peering into the black teardrop of his dead eye.

"Jesus." Then: "Is it true that one-eyed people see the world in only two dimensions?"

"No."

"But if something comes at you fast—"

"I played softball for a while. Never had a problem."

"It has to affect your perception."

"Happened a long time ago. You adjust. It's like nothing, now." Self-conscious, restless, Jack gets up and looks for his shirt.

"I was kind of hoping we could have dinner before you go. Just the two of us. No kids. Look, I shouldn't have—" Mona takes a deep breath. "*I'm* sorry. You didn't seem like, well, anyway, I should have told you right off that I had them, but . . . you know . . ."

Jack nods slightly. He's acting, but off-book now, and he's really not all that good at improv. "I like kids."

Mona puts her hands on her hips, her posture cocked. Studying him. She laughs nervously, and looks away.

"What?"

"Nothing."

"No."

"It's just. You sound . . . so . . . sincere." Then she catches herself and tries to backtrack, "Or, no, I mean—"

"I get what you mean."

"You must have known I had kids, Jack. You saw Zach and me yesterday night, by the pool."

Rewind, stop, fast-forward, stop, play: pool, voice, pale legs, doughy features, the suburban Scylla, Jack's misogynistic creature from the misogynistic lagoon of his personal hell. That was Mona?

"Is it a problem, my having kids?"

"No."

"Yet you're leaving."

Her look is more curious than hurt, and again it throws him off balance. Wind unfurls the curtains. "I just have to get back. Work. That was my, you know, agent."

"Yeah. You said that. ADR."

The next pause is decidedly awkward. Jack stretches to gently itch one of the long scratches on his back.

"Did I do that?"

"No." He says it too quickly, and his hand comes away too quickly from his back. "No."

"You call women *girls*."

He shrugs. "Same difference."

"No, it's not." Mona gets up, moves toward the door, finding the shadows. Jack stands, but stays where he is, looking around half-heartedly for his shirt, anticipating an outburst of emotion, maybe anger. Something. He can't see Mona at all, just her outline.

"I had fun. Really." Mona's voice is clear, unforgiving, almost happy. Jack doesn't know what the hell is going on. "Next time you get out this way, if I find out about it, I'll be insulted if you don't call me."

"Let's go to dinner, all of us. And your downsize Roger Clemens doesn't even have to make peace. He's just a kid, I come out here and, you know. Cut him some slack. He doesn't know me." Jack wishes he could see her face.

"He needs to know it's wrong," she says, and takes a moment more before confessing, "My kids have different fathers, Jack. I've never been married."

"That doesn't matter to me." Jack gives this his best reading. He has the sensation of floating, looking down on the room, not so much out-of-body as out-of-phase. "Look. Okay. Give me a minute here, and. I'll be right down. Okay? We'll go get a burger or pizza or something, all of us."

Guarded: "Okay."

Mona doesn't move. Jack burrows his mind into this final, outright lie, and tries to believe that he means it. Mona opens the door and walks out into the unkind light of the front porch. She turns. Now he can see her, and even in the awful mini-fluorescent wash, she's as beautiful as he remembers. She's still smiling, ever so slightly. Continuing her previous thought, "Or. You never know. I might come to L.A. Take the kids to see Disneyland."

"Happiest place on Earth," Jack says.

Mona lets the door close softly.

Jack is dropped into the darkness. He listens for Mona's footsteps on the stairs. Envisions her striding over the concrete, past
the solitary Joshua tree in the courtyard, toward her unit somewhere in the back of the motel complex. The sound of her leaving fades into the serenade of crickets and awkward rustle of a
small town settling into night.

After a couple of minutes, Jack's cigarette flares with one last
drag, sparks out in the ashtray on the phone desk, and Jack walks
out onto the balcony.

He stretches. There's tightness in his shoulders and down the
backs of his legs. To the west, among the swarming, stunted cactus trees, the motley lights of Yucca Valley taunt him with their
cheap illusion of stars that have fallen and broken and been scattered across the desert for him to find.

It takes no more than a minute for him to pack.

His car is still warm with the smell of baked cigarettes and
sunburnt upholstery leather.

Jack is gone when Mona and her kids cross the asphalt and climb
the stairs to the second floor. They waited about a half hour,
Mona's put on some makeup. Zach's hair is gel-spiked up, he's in
his good jeans, and he looks grimly resigned to the task ahead of
him. Carrie drags the stuffed bunny her Grammy gave her.

But by the time they reach the top of the stairs, Mona can't
believe she's actually playing this out. Some part of her wants
to believe that Jack's in the room, waiting. He said he'd come
down, but, okay, it is possible he's on the phone again. Something important. Maybe a part in a big movie, that they could
celebrate. It would be a good surprise, if that's what happened.

Instead, there's a strange man standing at Jack's room door,
knocking. They don't see him at first because the porch light is

out. Mona is sure that it was lit earlier. The man holds something down at his side, metal, from the way it catches the light. Mona takes her kids by the hands and walks tentatively closer.

"Can I help you?"

The man turns to face them.

Of course, Mona and her children wouldn't know Tory Geller.

seven

∎

Patrol cars from the cooperating jurisdictions are clustered on the back side of an I-10 overpass, so that the suspect will not see them until it's too late. There is a sign that points, as if prophetically, north to Joshua Tree, and south to Mecca. The suspect vehicle is known to be coming south. They wave the innocent on by; they have the make and color and license of the car they're looking for and down-traffic confirmation of its approach—a tip from some rock climbers who spotted the ebony Buick parked in a turnoff deep in the national park as they returned to Twenty-nine Palms; it was gone by the time the highway patrol helicopter did a flyover, but the split beam of its headlights were visible for miles on the winding road south to the interstate, giving the local authorities plenty of time to prepare their intercept.

"Edgar?" Voices clip through the static of shortwave radios. Souls lost in limbo.

"Forty-one is Code 7, over."

"Are you at IHOP?" Grace the dispatcher's lonely shout-out.

Sheriff's Deputy Arthur Soles has a pair of infrared night-vision binoculars he borrowed from the Yucca Valley cops to hunt coyotes a couple nights ago. He knows Deputy Edgar Vizcarra is actually having dinner at Denny's, because he was flashing discount coupons for a Moons Over My Hammmy all day.

"Edgar? Edgar, do you copy? Over." Grace sounds on edge. Disembodied, distant. Her husband is doing a second tour in Kandahar.

"What do you want, Grace, over?"

The barricade consists of two highway patrol black-and-whites, a park service SUV containing one huge, bored, curious ranger armed proudly with his own .45 Auto Mag, and a cream-colored Twentynine Palms Police Department station wagon parked across the southbound lane, and behind which the team waits, pensive. No lights are flashing.

"Those bear claws in the fridge? Are they—"

"Do not touch them, Grace. Repeat, do not touch them. They are spoken for. Over."

"Oh. Okay, okay. Copy that. Over."

Headlights from far down the highway flutter across the faces of the five officers: two highway patrolmen, crew cut, blond, buff, indistinguishable; Park Ranger Billy Petty, who wants to be a cop but can't pass the physical; and two lean San Bernardino Sheriff's Department deputies contracted to Twentynine Palms for its policing. Sweat stains bleed down the sides of their thick cotton winter-weight uniforms (the permanent-press summer khakis are on back order from a supplier in Riverside). The taller, more angular deputy, Soles, aims his impressive optics down the highway. Petty, who's been trying to quit chewing tobacco for six months, spits out of habit and rubs his boot over an imaginary splatter.

Deputy Vince Ng, first-generation Vietnamese and the pride of his Republican parents, shifts his weight, impatient. "That it?" Meaning the car.

Soles takes his time answering. "I believe so. Yup."

The approaching vehicle's bright lights dim. Engine whining as it slows. The officers all note the faint sound of rock music. One of the highway patrolmen deliberately lifts a high-powered rifle to the roof of his car, and steadies it, aiming.

Pounding, mind-stuffing music fills Jack's car as he glides through the lightless desert. He takes one last hit on the joint he's been nursing all night, opens both electric windows, flicks the joint out, letting it pinwheel brightly when it hits the pavement he's already left behind. Jack exhales, feeling the dope's resurgence. He took the back way out of town from Mona's motel, the lovely curving blacktop through the national park, all shadows and mystery in the dark. He pulled over at one point, climbed an easy rock pile, and lay spread-eagle, staring up at the canopy of stars, smoking his Mexican fatty and emptying his mind of Mona.

Hot wind whips through his hair, airing out the car. His eyes fix on the flashing red lights ahead, largely unconcerned. He hasn't done anything wrong, if you don't count skipping out on a lover, but that's not a crime, anyway, at least not one in the California Criminal Code. Up ahead, that's someone else's problem. It's an accident he'll pass.

He sees the flash before he hears the gunshot, clearly, out of rhythm with his music. The right front tire of his car is blown to pieces, the hubcap sent spinning off into the scrub as the Buick lurches sideways and bottoms out from the sheer torque of deceleration, throwing sparks from the chassis. Jack fights the spin, turns the wheel into it, "Shit—!" His heart pounding and his perception completely skewed now—am I high or is this really really really Jesus what the fuck—his car finally stopping some ten yards away from the barricade. Jack sits, stunned, music still pounding, pounding, while shapes emerge from the darkness on both sides of him, cops with guns. A scene he's played probably a hundred times. What the hell? And then an Asian officer throws open the driver's side door, and Jack's staring into the empty eternity of a double-barreled shotgun.

"GET DOWN ON THE GROUND, NOW!"

"What?"

Simultaneously, a highway patrolman lunges in through the other door, literally Jack's blind side, so he never even sees the man coming, and shoves Jack out, sprawling, onto the hot pavement of the highway.

And Jack's primary thought is: I can't let them know that I'm stoned.

Soles has a boot on the suspect's back, pressing him flat. He's reading the man his Miranda rights from a wallet-sized cheater card, while Ng frisks him and a spare highway patrolman aims a handgun at the suspect's head.

Ng looks through a sweat-stained leather Polo wallet. "Baylor, Jack Edward."

The suspect struggles to say something, "Can I, can I, can I, can I—"

"Shhhh." Ng flips the wallet onto the pavement, whips plastic twist-tie handcuffs out of his back pocket, and binds his suspect like a steer roper. The helpless man turns his head toward the thumping sounds to their left, watches Petty trying to beat the trunk of the Buick open with the butt of his rifle.

"Hey! Use the key!" Soles barks. "Use the key, Petty! Jesus Christ."

The trunk breaks, pops partway open under Petty's jackhammer persistence, but now it won't go up any farther and Petty has to lean in with a flashlight to unsuccessfully ascertain what's inside. Ng stares down at Baylor, Jack Edward, and makes no judgment except to marvel for the thousandth time how Petty ever got through even the National Park Service's officer training program however many years ago. Perhaps it was clerical error. Idly curious, Ng leaves Jack Edward Baylor immobile in the middle of the road, and joins the other officers gathering at the trunk.

Limp, ripped, Jack tries to sort out their voices, put them with the mere fragments of faces he's seen in the past thirty-six seconds, and can't.

"Don't touch anything. Somebody's going to want lab tests," Soles warns. A highway patrolman uses his foot to push the trunk lid up. "Nice work, Petty." It takes three tries.

"Empty." Soles observes, unnecessarily. "Damn it."

Jack wonders what they were expecting to find there. He wonders how much of his paranoia is justified. He waits for the mumbled, chagrined apologies for this misunderstanding. He wants to laugh, but thinks better of it.

Soles waves his flashlight over the car's interior, looking. Petty spits again. "Nothing in the car. No blood, no clothing, no mud and so forth. No sign of kids or nothing." Ng looks back gravely at Jack, and their eyes lock.

Blood? I didn't do anything, Jack wants to say, but his mouth is suddenly very, very dry.

Soles is back searching the trunk, as if he could have missed something in the dark corners. "Damn it."

The one named Petty drives the National Park Service SUV back toward Twentynine Palms. Ng sits up front, but keeps a constant eye on Jack in the backseat. Jack stares at the name tag: NG. Then up at the deputy's face. Ng just glares at him.

"Can I ask what—"

"No," Petty snaps. "Don't talk. No talking."

Jack just wants to know what is going to happen to his car, will they bring it to the station or what? Swiftly, a dope-fueled paranoia overtakes him. Will they pay for the damage to the trunk? Are they even cops? Maybe he won't push the point. Jack likes cops, he's played them on TV. He's gone on ride-alongs; they're good people. But he is beginning to feel just the littlest bit sorry for himself. This isn't worth it; he's going to miss the ADR session. Shit. What was he thinking? He could be having dinner with a couple of kids who want to stone him to death. Ha. Stone. He remembers, then, that there is no ADR session in L.A. That was the fiction. Which makes this, what, worse? Or ironic? Jack shifts his weight uncomfortably, his chest tight, his hands pinned behind him against the swayback vinyl seat. He looks out at the night and sighs.

Faces.

Whitewashed by headlights, faces, staring. Jack recognizes among them the bartender from the Roundup Room at the Rancho Del Dorotea, that tough, old marine gunner who hit on Mona, two of the cholla ladies, still wet from a swim, both in swimsuits with little hip-hiding skirts.

He imagines he's them, seeing him, Jack's face, trapped behind the glass of the SUV window, staring out with an expression of utter confusion, like a lizard who finds himself captured and imprisoned in an empty peanut butter jar with a couple of holes punched in the lid.

The SUV parks between a Morongo Valley Volunteer Fire Department rescue vehicle and three Twentynine Palms Police sedans. Jack is hauled out and led down the breezeway, into the motel courtyard where Soles catches up with them. Ng keeps a firm hold on one of Jack's arms, Soles hangs back, Petty has disappeared.

"I don't know what's going on," Jack says.

Nobody will answer.

The pool glows aquamarine from the underwater lights. A new cluster of cops, firefighters, paramedics, and a few motel guests crowd the stairs to the second floor. They step aside as Ng and Jack approach, eyes on Jack as the cops take his arms and guide him up the stairs. Jack wonders why firefighters wear their firefighting gear even when they know there's not a fire. It looks heavy. Don't they get hot?

Another cop steps aside to let them enter Jack's former motel room. It's a mess. Furniture is out of place, chairs overturned, the screen of the television has been smashed in, and there is blood everywhere.

And there is blood. Everywhere.

Streaked in desperate handsprings on the wall near the front door. Spattered across the carpet, the bed sheets, the glass balcony doors, and thin white curtains. Blood pooled on the bathroom's linoleum floor. Blood smeared across the shower door. A bloody towel. A bloody pale blue plush toy bunny.

Jack's knees buckle, and he throws up.

Ng jumps back, too late. "Thank you." Disgusted, he starts to drag Jack out. Petty appears again, tries to help, but only gets hold of one leg so, awkwardly, they hurry Jack back through the door and out into the hot night, to hobble—nearly falling—down the stairs and dump him into a planter filled with ice plants. His shirt has been pulled halfway off. Both deputies make mental notes of Mona's fingernail scratches on Jack's back as he heaves, on hands and knees, until there's nothing left inside him.

"Where'dja bury 'em, asshole?" Petty asks, tired. "Tell us where she and the kids is, we can all go home get some sleep."

Jack looks up. He doesn't understand the question. His eyes are watering. He sees, across the courtyard, distorted by the heat and his tears and the sharp descent from his marijuana high, Deputy Soles talking to the bartender and the cholla woman who called herself Paula and knew him for the asshole he is. The marine is behind them.

Paula keeps pointing at Jack, and talking.

eight

■

Again: the cigarette, end up on a tabletop, burning itself down to a stub.

Jack stares at it, wondering: habit or affectation? He's never felt so tired before. Over his shoulder, he knows, Ng and a Twentynine Palms police detective named Booker or Cooke are standing in the corridor outside this pleasant interrogation room, both staring in at Jack's sweat-soaked back, through a window.

"What did you do with the kids?"

Jack looks up and across the table at Adam Beasely, the San Bernardino County public defender for the Twentynine Palms/ Joshua Tree basin. Beasely has a fat, red, sirloin face marbled with the varicose veins of a raging alcoholic. He's sweating hard. "Did you kill the kids, too, Jack? I will need to know that, right up front."

"No you won't." Jack folds his hands. "I did a *Law & Order* once where I played a public defender. I gave a long speech about

how it wasn't necessary for him to tell me whether he was innocent or guilty, and that, in fact, if he told me he was guilty I
would be required to factor that into my defense strategy since
I could not mount a case for innocence for a client I knew was
guilty. So I told my client, or rather the guy playing the client in
the episode, to tell me what happened and then we'd figure out
what to do."

Beasely sighs. "Okay. What happened?"

"I said goodbye to my friend Mona. I got in my car. I started
driving back to L.A. The cops stopped me and cuffed me and
brought me back here." Beasely stares at Jack emptily. "I smoked
the ass-end of a blunt in the car before they arrested me," Jack
confesses. "In case it comes up."

"Are you a regular drug user? Maybe you don't remember
what happened because you were stoned."

"Innocence. Foreign concept for you, Mr. Beasely?"

"I'll level with you, Jack. I can't defend you if you killed the
kids. I apologize."

"Can't or won't?"

"Okay." He's chagrined. "Won't."

"I didn't—"

"—no, you're right, never mind—"

"—kill anybody."

"Don't say anything, not important, mea culpa. I shouldn't
ask, and more to the point, Jack, it doesn't really matter since,
under the law, you are presumed innocent and so forth and my
task, as you say, is to hear you out, to listen without prejudice
and then, God willing, together we can work to achieve the best
possible result given the crime, circumstances, evidence against
you, and . . . so forth."

"That was my speech," Jack says.

Beasely stares at Jack, sad. "I doubt I can do this under any circumstances, though," Beasely admits, but presses forward. "What was your speech?"

"No, forget it. Nothing." Jack is still coming down hard off his high. He has moments of clarity, followed by suffocating paranoia, followed by resonant doubt that whatever clarity he experiences isn't, in fact, more pot-fueled illusion. Jack repeats to Beasely, "I didn't kill anyone." Jack knows that he didn't, and yet the dogged conviction with which everyone else seems to think he did, and the very fact of his arrest rattles him and sets off another round of paranoia. Innocence doesn't seem to be enough. What else? What else?

"People, in the motel, heard an argument," Beasely is saying. "Folks saw you and Mona Malloy together. She informed the desk clerk you all were going out for dinner. That would be you and Ms. Malloy and the children, you see."

"I was already gone."

"Driving away."

"Yes."

"Didn't say goodbye."

"No, I did. Sort of. But."

"But what?"

Jack wants to laugh, but not because it's funny. Yeah, Jack, but what? "I don't know."

"You don't know why you left, or why you left without saying goodbye?"

"No. Yes."

"According to your driver's license you only have legal sight in one eye."

"That's right." Beasely looks at him, trying to guess which one is the good one. "I have trouble with commitment," Jack adds, hoping that this explains something. The room spins. He closes his eyes.

"Because of your condition?"

Jack shakes his head. "No. Because I'm a shithead. To quote any of my ex-girlfriends."

Beasely looks down at his scrawled notes. "The victim had a record. Did you know that?"

It takes Jack a moment to connect the dots and understand that the public defender is talking about Mona.

"I don't—"

"She did some hard time," Beasely explains.

Jack frowns. Prison? "For what?"

Beasely looks up. "What?"

"What did she do?"

"I don't know." Beasely scans his notes on Mona. "Um. Manslaughter." He looks up. "Hey. Maybe you did this in self-defense."

"She *killed* somebody?"

"Maybe she tried to whack you, and . . ." It's as if Jack isn't there. "Ahhh, no, the kids," Beasely muses grimly, "how to explain the kids, though. That doesn't track with manslaughter. Always back to the kids, see?"

Jack says it deliberately, "Mr. Beasely, who did Mona kill?"

Beasely looks up at him again. "Were you drinking, too, Jack?" he asks, as if hopefully. "Sometimes, you know, strong libations will cause a man to, uhhh . . . black out. As I said, maybe you can't remember what you've done."

Frustrated, Jack finally picks up the cigarette, puffs on it. Puts it down. "Would it help you to defend me, Mr. Beasely, if I told you I was drinking?"

"No. See . . . the kids? That's, yes, that's the clincher, Jack, I'm sorry to say. The kids, well, see, from my perspective, from where I sit and I sit here across from you, Jack, the kids trump every suit." Beasely's hands are trembling. His left fingers are cupped, as if holding the drink he needs terribly, the more he thinks about it. "I'm going to need to recuse myself. I hold an irresolvable prejudice, I'm sorry, it's probably contempt, oh it will cost me, but they'll send out for a P.D. from Indio or, I don't know, some damn place. I apologize, but you understand."

"I DIDN'T KILL ANYBODY!" Jack turns and screams at the cops in the window: "I DIDN'T KILL ANYBODY!"

The cigarette falls over, scattering its tiny tower of ashes. Ng and the D.A. move away from the door and disappear. Beasely mops his face with his hand. Wipes it on his pants. He looks thirsty. His tongue thick.

"Of course you didn't. Just keep saying that." Beasely licks his chapped lips. "But try to remember what happened, you need a better explanation of what happened."

"I told you what happened," Jack says. "I—"

"*I* was drinking, Jack," Beasely confesses.

"You what?"

"Gin. When they called . . . tonight, earlier . . . I was drinking gin, I'll admit to that. And apologize for it. My head's not as clear as it should be. That's—well, okay, here it is—I'm not afraid to tell you I am not at all thinking clearly right now and you have the right to a clear-thinking attorney, because these are most serious charges."

The public defender heaves himself up, away from the table. "Perhaps, look, if they can't find anybody else, uh, hell, tomorrow. I'll come back. Because, shit. Fuck. They're not gonna, they're not gonna. Find. Anybody. *Shit*. You can see I'm right." He half bows, extremely remorseful, snatches up his old briefcase and hurries out of the room.

nine

■

Eventually Jack is in shackles, actual shackles, paraded by the park cop, Petty, through a sprawling room of desks and cubicles under the white canopy of a fluorescent plastic panel drop ceiling, to a metal door that opens noiselessly and clicks shut behind them revealing a small and sanitary cinderblock sanctuary of white walls and stainless steel partitions defining three dimly lit holding cells.

Petty triggers a switch that opens a door to one of the cells, then leads Jack in and unlocks the restraint that's been chafing his left wrist.

"You're shaking," Petty says.

Jack breaks a nervous smile. "I'm a little scared. Yeah."

"Oh."

A sudden movement catches Jack's eye. The girl in the sundress, Jack can't remember her name, is in the far cell, staring back at Jack and Petty as if they were a TV game show. Her look asks the question, so Jack geeks back at her, defensive: "I don't belong here, it's all some sick joke."

The girl just blinks, noncommittal.

Jack turns away, starting to relax now—the girl in the cell makes him feel like he hasn't gone completely crazy, it's just this whacky desert town where anybody can wind up in detention; maybe this will be one of those amazing episodes that happens to you and later you entertain people in auditions with an animated retelling of it. Jack turns, expecting Petty to remove the rest of the shackles, but Petty lifts the rig, clips the left handcuff instead to the crossbar in the cell door, and then drives his fist into Jack's ribcage, punching the wind out of him. Pain explodes in colors that blind Jack momentarily in his good eye. He sags. Petty hits him again, this time just under the shoulder blade. And again. And again.

At some point, Petty's wheezing, labored breathing takes Jack away from the searing hot agony of the beating. Out of body, Jack realizes that the park cop isn't in very good shape at all. Petty should work out, Jack thinks. Well, okay, maybe the guy lifts weights, but without any aerobic complement. Aerobics are essential. Jack can think of several places Petty could go in L.A. and get a good workout for under $39.95 a month, if he shopped around.

In her cell, the girl hasn't moved. Maybe she's not even there. Later, Jack will not be able to say how long the beating lasted. Seconds? Minutes? Maybe the girl will know.

Panting like he's run a marathon, Petty stops, lets Jack sag into his shoulder, holding him up while he catches his breath. Jack can't explain or comprehend why his legs aren't working; the universe has imploded and become the lump of air in his windpipe that won't go into his lungs. Petty unlocks the shackles from the cell bar and Jack's feet, then uses them to whipsaw Jack into the cell. Jack skids to his knees in front of the low-flow toilet. Petty grabs the hair on the back of Jack's head and plunges his face into the deodorant-blue water. Jack flails, helpless, gagging on disinfectant as Petty frees Jack's right wrist and lets the restraint fall to the floor.

"We're gonna play bad cop, bad cop." Petty's voice is underwater. He pulls Jack's head up so hard it breaks the toilet seat away from the bowl.

Jack gasps for air. He doesn't think Petty will kill him, but suspects that there may yet be worse things that can happen. He squeaks in a voice he doesn't recognize, "I didn't do it! Oh, Jesus, I didn't do it! Whatever, whatever, look, whatever happened had nothing to do with me—"

Petty jams Jack's head into the water again. "You got us by the short hairs, Mr. Baylor. No doubt about that." He yanks Jack's head up again, lets go. Jack falls over on his side, coughing. Limp. Petty purrs: "Without those little bodies we don't really have a case. Eventually you could even be released. That's how rule of law works in this country. We got no way to know where you put 'em. Thousand square miles of nothing out there, and, oh, maybe the slightest chance somebody'll stumble on 'em, big chance nobody ever will, ever. And you walk free. That your hole card here?"

"You didn't find bodies?"

"Darn you." Petty is going to punch him again.

"No. I can. Phone call—please—"

"Will you—I mean—you don't think you'll be able to live with yourself? No sir. The guilt, Jack. The outright horror, I mean."

Now Jack knows, as panic twists bile from his stomach, they will kill him. They want to kill him. Pain surges up on him, from every part of his body, so intense he has to concentrate to form the words: "I want . . . to make a phone call. I get a phone call."

Petty leans in very close to Jack's ear, his breath strangely cold and liquid. "No, you get twenty-four hours to scour your pathetic soul for the courage to own up to the unspeakable thing you have done, lover boy. Then, I personally am going to use your belt to hang you by the neck until you're dead, in this very cell, and we'll call it suicide."

"I didn't kill her." Jack's no longer sure he's saying anything. His mouth moves, but he can't hear himself.

Petty picks up the shackles. Jack just lies curled up on the floor, eyes closed, coughing.

"I don't believe you, Mr. Baylor. I don't." Petty cuts his eyes to the girl in her cell. "You didn't see this."

The girl is just a shadow, blind and mute.

The cop walks out. The cell door closes. The metal door back into the squad room glides open, displacing air that Jack can feel, cool, across his forehead, and then the door clicks shut. Jack's whole body shakes. He's crying. The tears burn his lips.

Jack doesn't remember how he got off the floor and onto the cot, or how long he's been here. He lies motionless, staring up at the ceiling of the holding cell, where tiny patches of mildew have begun to breed in the corners. Jack's side is numb, and if he moves, it feels like skin is ripping off his ribs.

A moth beats its wings on the naked ceiling lightbulb just outside the cell. Whether the moth is in front of the lightbulb, on the lightbulb, or behind the lightbulb, Jack can't immediately tell without moving, and moving is, for the moment, out of the question. But he knows from experience that the moth is doomed.

When he can hold himself upright again, Jack puts his feet to the floor and stands like an old man and begins to walk forced laps, back and forth, across around the cell, one arm pressed stiffly to his side. He can't sleep, there is nothing to do, and he wills himself not to think about Mona or the motel room or what may have happened there. He walks slowly, back and forth, five shuffling paces from wall to wall. Lines of dialogue from scenes he has played come back to him in exclamations, but for the moment, he can't remember the scenes.

"I believe you." The girl in the sundress is standing at the bars of her cell, looking through the empty cell between them at Jack, who'd forgotten she was there.

"I'll testify. I'll say what they did to you. I'm not scared of them." She hesitates. "They're wrong to do that to you."

Jack stares at her. "What are you doing in here?"

"Supposedly my parents're coming to pick me up." She waits awhile to continue. "I sort of ran away."

"I've forgotten your name."

"And the cops think they're teaching me a lesson." Rachel continues. "Rachel," she says.

"That's a nice name. Rachel."

"Yeah, it sucks, I hate it."

The burned moth flutters weakly, near dead, on the concrete floor beyond the cell door. A strangely companionable silence grows. Divorced of the setting.

Jack resumes his painful pacing.

The girl sits on her cot and watches.

Sometime later—how much time passes? Two hours? Five?—Jack sits down again, head in his hands, staring at the toilet. The seat is broken away, and water dribbles incessantly into the bowl from a leaky seal.

When Jack's mother was dying—her lungs turned to paper, her heart big and useless—he would sit by her bed holding her hand, while the toilet in the next room would run and run because the flange or something was broken and Jack's father didn't fix it because Mom wanted the sound of it, needed the fact of it, the promise of it, because as long as water was running she was still here and part of this imperfect world, connected to the past and the possibility of a future in which the leak got fixed. With death a sure thing, yawning endless before her, Jack's mother's mind couldn't wrap itself around the astonishing truth that she would be here and then not, that she could exist and then cease. And that her God would allow it.

They're not going to kill me, Jack thinks. Not in front of the girl. They're just trying to scare me.

Although two hours ago—five?—he would have disbelieved anything that has happened since.

The sad part is, it's working, Jack admits.

But what if they think he did it and they can't prove it-because he really didn't do it, which they can't know—would they kill him in some headlong scrum for justice? It's the plot of a movie Jack has seen, or read, or read for. And if he tells them he did it, if he caves and confesses to the cops, or deputies, or fucking park ranger, sure maybe they won't kill him now, but he'll face a death warrant for the crime he didn't commit.

"Hey. Mister. Baylor."

Jack's thoughts tumble, bingo balls in a wire-mesh cage, filling his card without a winner.

"Jack. Excuse me."

The moth stops moving. Decisions, unequivocal decisions that unspool concrete consequences, have never been Jack's strong suit.

He stands up and unbuttons his jeans.

"Oh God," Rachel says, "now what. What are you doing?"

* * *

"Toilet's busted!"

In the police station day room, a lone sentry, Petty, naps, head on his arms, at a vacant desk. Perhaps dreaming that he's a cop. Water bangs in the pipes overhead, and the suspect in the holding cell, Mr. Baylor, is screaming: "YOUR TOILET'S BUSTED!!!"

Petty wakes up with an unpleasant start, knocks over his Styrofoam cup of cold coffee. He blinks in the glare of unnatural light. Squints at the clock: midnight and a half. He should have gone home, doesn't really have any jurisdiction here. Petty pushes himself up out of the chair.

The sideways Styrofoam cup rocks on the edge of the desk as he walks back toward the cells. Pale brown coffee drips down onto the carpeting.

Water flows out of the toilet and across the concrete floor of Jack's cell. Petty has to slosh through it. Jack sits inside, on the cot, feet up.

Rachel stands on her cot, too. "Gross. Can I leave now?"

"What'd you do to it?" Petty asks Jack, ignoring the runaway minor.

"I took a whiz."

Petty looks down at his shoes. "Yeah. Well I'm not gonna fix it. How's that sit with you?"

Jack nods. "Okay."

"Gross!" from the other cell.

Petty looks at his own feet again, at the water flooding across the concrete toward the rest of the station house. Quietly he cusses, something Jack imagines Petty ordinarily would never do. Jack watches as the big man sloshes back to an electric panel and—wiping his feet dry first—triggers a switch that opens the cell door.

Jack stays on the cot, watching Petty come back.

"What'd you, plug the drain?"

Jack says nothing. Maybe Petty cusses on the job, but never at home. His wife, if he has one, doesn't know. Petty's in the cell, stooping, groping in the water, pulls up the wad of mattress batting Jack stuffed into the floor drain. The water begins to recede, but the toilet keeps overflowing.

"This ain't helping you, Jack."

"Nothing's helping me."

"How about the truth?"

"Tried it."

Petty sees what's wedged in the bottom of the swirling toilet. Rolls up his sleeve. Reaches in.

Jack steps lightly into the water. He raises the broken toilet seat he was concealing under his leg, grabs it with two hands and brings it down with a sodden, slapping sound, onto the target of Petty's declined head and neck, hitting the big park cop so hard the seat splinters.

"Whoa," Rachel hisses. "Did you kill him?"

Petty drops face-first into the water, still clutching the soggy pair of Jack's underwear he had just retrieved. The toilet calms and drains.

Swallowing panic, Jack bolts from the cell, to leave.

"Hey!" Rachel calls after him.

He stops, comes back into the cell and takes Petty's gun from its holster.

"What about me?"

Jack wonders if it's loaded, or how to tell. He assumes it is. It has to be. And again he walks out.

"Jack?" Again he stops, and comes back into his cell.

He puts the gun on the bed, squats, and rolls Petty over. Puts his face close to Petty's lips, making sure the ranger is still breathing. He is. Jack rocks back on the balls of his feet. His whole body aches. His heart pounds. He straightens up.

"Take me with you."

Jack looks at Rachel blankly. "I can't. I'm sorry."

He gets all the way to the door this time before he comes back again, into the cell, for the gun he put down on the bed.

"Look," Rachel is saying, pleading, really, "come on, Jack, give me a break. I can't go back home, okay? Please?"

At the cell block doorway, Jack opens the silent steel door and peers out into the station room. He reaches back, punches the electric switch on the box on the wall, just like Petty did. The cell door closes. Petty doesn't move.

"Please." Rachel is crying.

Jack says, "They think I killed people, Rachel. You do not want to be a part of this."

Rachel shakes with emotion, "My dad—" She hesitates, doesn't want to say it; bites her lips, her eyes plead with Jack: Come on, come on, connect the dots, figure it out. "Why do you think I ran away?"

Jack studies her, exhales loudly, hesitates, then punches the switch for her cell door, and it rolls open. Rachel hurries out, sneakers slapping through the toilet water.

"We go out together, then we split up. You can't be with me, it's not safe."

Rachel slips out past him into the day room before he can say anything else. There's no one here now. Jack can hear a dispatcher talking, somewhere down the corridor. Rachel grabs his hand and pulls him through the doorway.

"You're almost old enough to be him."

"Who?"

"My dad."

They head away from the dispatcher's voice, toward the back of the station, following Lucite exit signs. A sleepy-eyed cop comes out of a men's room. Jack smiles, panicking. Rachel squeezes his hand.

"I won't do it again, Daddy," Rachel says to Jack in her quavery voice. "I promise I won't." The cop nods dully at them, barely registering the passing domestic crisis.

Headlights pin Jack and Rachel in high beams, then drift away as a car pulls into the parking lot, power-steering complaining miserably. Men laughing. Music on a radio. Classic rock of the eighties. The night air is hot and syrupy.

They walk away from the building, away from the street. At a barbed wire fence on the edge of city police property, Jack spreads the span with his foot and one hand, helping Rachel keep her head down with the other as she slips through, then climbs through after her, catching his shirt and ripping it. They slip-slide down an embankment into a dry arroyo littered with garbage and beer cans and old refrigerators that glow like carcasses in the milky-white moonlight. Jack's not thinking too much. He's moving. He's in motion.

Jack throws the gun away.

"What did you do that for?" Rachel hisses. "We may need that."

But Jack knows he has no use for it. He's only fired a gun once, a long time ago, with his Uncle Lloyd, at that shooting range outside of Wichita. It was a .22 rifle, and he never hit the target.

"There is no *we*. You're on your own now, Rachel. You're on your own."

She says nothing. She just stares at him, silently.

Jack wants to stop now. He's tired. His ribs ache. He wants to cry. He wants to imagine Mona still back at Rancho Del Dorotea motel, kids asleep on the sofa, waiting for him, realizing ruefully what a worthless shitheel he is and promising herself to be more careful next time.

If he could just hear the sound of his knock on her door. If he could just get held, again, by her fierce eyes, even if only in utter contempt.

Jack sighs, looks up at the moon, a hole in the darkness. He closes his eyes. Then he motions for Rachel to follow him.

They run, together, moving away, toward the dark, empty desert.

ten

■

Joshua trees, forever. Surreal. Arms upraised, an insurrection, defiant. Thousands of prickly rioters.

Under the brutal sun.

Larry Mahan boots scuffle through the desert dust, chipped stone, and grass chaff. They scramble up a rocky slope. Dirty sneakers follow close behind, light and agile.

The desert spread out hot and bleak behind him, Jack's shirt is off and his sunburned body shines, slick with sweat.

"Maybe you should stop."

Jack keeps climbing.

"You look like you're going to have a heart attack or something.

"Fine. Kill yourself," she adds.

"I'm good," Jack says.

He reaches the crest of the broken rock mountain and stalls out, lungs heaving, wiping the stinging moisture from his eyes to look down across a Mojave valley cut and scarred by a snake of asphalt that vanishes on a treeless horizon.

"How old are you, anyway?"

Jack turns to answer Rachel, but never even gets his mouth open before another voice is with them.

"Gotcha."

The two marines from the Roundup Room, now in sweat-stained Desert Storm fatigues and full packs, stand just behind Rachel, aiming their automatic rifles at Jack, cracking gum. Their name tags say MILLER and HUDSON. In their desert camo, they're interchangeable.

Rachel jumps, startled. "Fuck me!"

"Dude." Hudson to Miller: "Getaloada the trash-talking tween."

"Can you hear this?" Rachel asks, showing them an extended middle finger held parallel to the ground, "or should I turn it up?"

Jack's heart sinks. "Yeah. You got me." Now what?

"Never heard us coming," gloats the one tagged Miller. He's got weight-room shoulders and basically no neck.

"No, I didn't."

Hudson smiles. "We been tailing you for, minimum, like two clicks, brah."

"Guy from shrimp night," says Miller with recognition.

Hudson stares blankly. "Dude, what?"

"Neurosurgeons," Rachel says to Jack.

"Shrimp night at the Dorotea. I remember the boots," Miller explains. "Dude, I covet those boots."

Relief surges through Jack as he nods, "That's right."

"He was working that little spinner in the green pumps." Now Hudson's on the same page. "Howyadoin?"

"Okay," says Jack. "This is my sister."

"I 'member."

"Whatchou doin' the hell out here?"

"Gee," Rachel deadpans, "I dunno."

Jack adds, quickly, "What about you guys?"

Hudson makes a face. "Survival hike. Ten days, full pack, canteen, and two days' dry rations."

"Get us ready for the sandbox."

"Except for the total absence of Hajjis and IEDs." They bump fists.

"Bitch and a half," Miller observes, grinning. "Or would be. But? Meeting our girlfriends down at Highway 61, goin' to Mexicali for a last few days of unofficial R&R. Come back, walk a bit, workupasweat, and when the recon choppers pick us up, nobody's the wiser."

"Fewer and prouder," Rachel says.

They all laugh. Hudson takes a pack of cigarettes out of his pocket, offers them around. Rachel declines. All three men smoke, gazing out at the desert.

Jack feels like someone has filled him with helium and he's floating thirty feet above the ground. Time has stopped. Everything has stopped.

"Hey," Hudson says suddenly. "You get a taste of that spinner?" Jack shrugs—a "not in front of my sister" gesture—and smokes. Rachel stares at him. "Yes, he did," she says flatly.

The marines nudge each other. Of course he did. Otherwise everything they believe about life and purpose comes crashing down and they are just a couple of jarheads in the high desert, a few weeks out from carrying fifty-seven pounds of prescribed deadweight that might as well be their lives because some turkey-necked Pentagon strategist who spent the last Gulf War stranded at Diego Garcia counting and recounting MREs thinks it will shore up the timbers of democracy.

"How far you walking—"

"Jack," Jack says.

"Jack." Miller gestures to himself. "Tommy Miller," and to his grinning companion, "Tommy Hudson."

"Tommies," says Hudson.

"Convenient," says Rachel.

"How far you walking today, Jack?" Miller asks.

Jack thinks for a moment. "How far is Mexicali?"

The marines grin.

eleven

■

"Hey. He's an actor," Ng holds up Jack's SAG card.

Ng is taking apart Jack's leather Polo wallet with a pair of forensic tweezers, while Soles watches. An evidence baggy filled with shredded pink pistachio shells is on the desk in front of him; Soles and Ng have side-by-side workstations in the Twentynine Palms police station. They're sheriff's department, assigned out of the Morongo Basin substation; San Bernardino County's been providing contract law enforcement services to the city since 1988. Soles thinks his posting is a punishment for having briefly dated the sheriff's frisky Victorville niece. Ng thinks that's bullshit; the sheriff needed fourteen bodies to staff the station and probably literally pulled names out of his size-six hat.

Petty, behind them, backward on the chair and with a two-dollar Rite Aid ice pack on the side of his head, tries to pretend he doesn't know they want to ignore him.

"Your big city jails don't have seats on the stainers," Petty opines. "They got special jail cell toilets. Safety first. I wrote a interagency district-wide memo on this very subject of Hidden Weapons Among Us, but evidently nobody read it, and here we are."

"Driver's license?" Soles asks Ng.

Ng finds it: "Jack Edward Baylor. Los Angeles address." He flips the laminated ID to Soles.

Soles touches the red dot pasted on the license. "Organ donor."

"I could potentially sue the county for liability," Petty says.

Ng unfolds a leathery snapshot stuck in the corner of the wallet's cash pocket. It's a photograph of Jack in a tuxedo; he stands next to a bride and groom. Hannah and Tory Geller are the lucky couple. Everyone's smiling.

"Frankly, I mean, it's pretty much pure malicious neglect nobody thought to pull that porcelain abomination the hell out of there years back. Liability, neglect. Infliction of emotional distress."

"Petty," Soles says, "what you've got is the lump of abject stupidity upside your head."

"I'd like to of seen you in there, Soles. I'd like to of seen what you'd of done, you might be dead." Petty's feelings are hurt. "Give a criminal a weapon, and—any weapon—and the opportunity to use it—well, you just start there and . . ."

Soles stares at Petty, waiting for the conclusion of a thought that has already run its course. Ng sorts through Jack's cash, business cards, random receipts. The cigarette lighter. One nickel. A couple of condoms.

"Ribbed," Soles notes. "Is that really a useful feature?"

"He's gonna go back home," Ng says.

"You think?"

"I do."

"Okay. I'll bite. Why?"

"Vaccination card. He's got a cat." Ng holds up a folded rabies vaccination receipt.

"Nice work, Holmes."

"You mean *homes*," Petty says, crabby. "Jesus. Get it right."

Nobody's listening to him.

twelve

■

In the hot shade of the wide awnings of the Gato Verde Cafe, an INS border agent in a short-sleeved uniform drops money in a battered vending machine, opens the vent, and withdraws the late edition of the *San Diego Tribune*. He stands for a moment, perusing the unfolded front page, possibly wondering if the place where rebels and troops exchanged gunfire is in the Middle East or Africa, then quickly shuffles it front to back for the sports section. The Padres have dropped another one-run game.

He does not bother with the small item about a grisly murder in the high desert, or the prime Person of Interest's audacious midnight escape; he does notice the faint reflection of a man's face in the window of the vending machine, and looks up to discover the self-same fugitive pictured in a tiny reprint of an actor's head shot staring out at him from a corner window booth in the café, trying to read the headlines broken by the man's thick, clutching fingers.

But the INS man hasn't seen Jack's picture.

"Come on, Tommy. He'll do it if you do it."

"I never said that."

"You did," Hudson's girlfriend insists. "Both of us heard it."

The agent folds up his paper and walks to his khaki-colored Jeep Cherokee. Just before getting in, he turns, frowning, to look back at Jack with the expression of someone who's seen something he should remember. He smiles. Jack smiles back, then turns his attention to the Tommies and their girlfriends, Brandee and Vicko, sitting with him in the window booth. Jack sips his water, crunching the ice with his teeth. Willing himself not to look out the window again to see if the INS man has left. Rachel's working on a patty melt, quiet and shy in the presence of older girls. And these are, Jack decides in his mulish, ongoing debate with the resonance of Mona, girls.

"You guys suck" is the gist of their complaint about the jarheads.

"They're doubling up on us, bud," Hudson says to Miller, unperturbed.

"Semper fi," says Miller, touching fists with Hudson.

"Semper fi," says Hudson.

"What has an IQ of forty-two?" Vicko asks.

"Forty marines and their CO," Brandee answers.

Brandee is plush and padded, Vicko sleek and feral and wearing an I GOT HAMMERED AT HUSSONG'S T-shirt that's two sizes too small. They've already exhausted the requisite recognize-Jack-from-somewhere conversation—yes, television, *Wildwood* or that one time on *Law & Order SVU*—it was a long, hot, open ride across the desert and the air-conditioned quiet of the café has made the marines and their girls cranky in the wake of a lame joke about quick Mexican weddings.

The Gato Verde is big on Mexicano-ironic decor, lots of cat-

motif black-velvet art, jalapeño string lights. The corner booth
is upholstered in Naugahyde, the only green booth in the café. A
perky waitress collects their empty plates, balancing them on one
arm as she rips the meal check off its pad.

"Anything else?" She's too cheerful.

Brandee ignores her, stares icily at Hudson. "I don't want to
go across the border unless it's to get married."

"Sweet Jesus."

"What about you, honey?" The waitress looks at Rachel, who
smiles politely and shakes her head.

"Brandee, get serious. We elope? Your mother freaks."

"You don't give a flavorful fuck about what my mother
thinks."

"You know she will! And I get blamed! No. This is one area
where we do not frog the bitch."

Miller nudges Vicko. "See what you started?"

Brandee has a bite to her. "Grow up, Tommy. And don't call
my mother a bitch."

The waitress puts the check down. "Whenever you're ready."
She flees. Jack reaches for the bill.

"I've got this."

Vicko puts her hand on Jack's. "No—we'll split it." She looks
at Miller. "Won't we, Honey?" Hudson is completely content to
let Jack pay.

"You drove," Jack says, gently pulling his hand, and the check,
to his corner of the booth. "I want to do something for you guys."
Jack reaches for his wallet, surprised that he doesn't find it, and
remembers he doesn't have one anymore. The cops took it.

Rachel is watching him, probably way ahead of him, he suspects, since she doesn't have her backpack anymore either. They
trade looks, she shrugs, out of ideas.

"Maybe," Brandee says sharply to Hudson, "I just don't feel like spending another weekend watching you guys get drunk as pigs and drag us from strip joint to strip joint."

"Major turn on, for us," Vicko tag-teams, "really."

"We're not gonna do that." Miller looks hurt. "We got tickets to the bullfights."

"Jack." Hudson touches Jack's arm. "You okay, man?"

Vicko gestures, frowning. "Something wrong with your eye?" Jack ignores her, says, "I lost my wallet." There's silence, during which he has time to reset, and make a better, second reading of the line: "I lost my wallet." His eyes avoid contact with anyone. It's just a choice. He could sell it a hundred different ways, but this feels right.

"Shit." Hudson has, no doubt, lost his wallet many times, in many bars. "Where? Back in Twentynine Palms?"

Brandee's voice is still high and tight. "I'm not going to a bull-fight."

Miller winces, with mock pain. "Geez, come on, girl—when we get married? I want it to be magic. You know? The real deal: dress uniform and French champagne. Cut the cake with a sword, garter belts, satin and lace and shit."

Brandee stares at him. "Are you proposing?" Miller's slight hesitation earns Brandee's scowl. She pushes out of the booth and walks away, past the postcard racks, and out the door.

"Fuck!" Miller looks at Jack and Hudson and Vicko. He understands that he has to go after her. "No—hey—Brandee!"

Hudson peels two twenties out of his billfold and lays them on the check. He winks at Jack and Rachel, nudges for Vicko to "Start motivating for the exit, sweet thang."

When Jack gets outside, he's welcomed by a blast of desert-baked air and the sight of Brandee angrily heaving military backpacks out of the fire-red convertible Sunbird that brought them all out of the Mojave. Miller tries reasoning with his girlfriend in a low voice, but patience is failing him. Hudson, Vicko, and Jack watch, keeping safely distant.

"I'm not going if she's not going," Vicko tells Hudson.

Hudson looks for support from Jack, but Rachel comes out of the double doors behind them, face wet and pink from restroom soap and paper towels, a toothpick in her teeth. "We've got to go back and find your wallet," Rachel says deliberately. "Don't we, Jack?"

Jack's head is nodding, but his thoughts are tangled. Mexico was never more than an impulse. Jack just wanted to put some distance between himself and the Rancho Del Dorotea. For the past twenty minutes he's been calculating who, back in L.A., might be able to help him. Ordinarily he'd run to Tory, but first he needs to know what Hannah has said, and done. "You guys have been great," he tells Hudson. "Thanks for the ride. And lunch. Really appreciated."

"Dude. Mexico."

"I know."

"How you gonna get back without any money?"

Jack shrugs. "I can get my agent to wire me some. Or something. Don't sweat it, we'll be fine."

"Do it now, brah." Hudson digs a cell phone out of his pocket and puts it into Jack's hands. "Otherwise I'm gonna worry."

"You don't even know me."

"Yeah. So?"

Vicko shakes her head, watching Brandee and Miller arguing with each other. "Love sucks."

Not far away, on the edge of a parking lot, is an old glassed-in phone booth that shakes like it's coming apart when Jack pushes open the door to find some cover from the incessant wind. Rachel has followed him. "What if the police have tracked down your agent?" she says. "What if they've wiretapped his phone?"

Jack stares at her. "Wiretapping is illegal."

"Patriot Act. Ever heard of it?"

"I'm not a terrorist."

"You're not a murderer, either, but look where that got us. Lemme see." She takes the phone from him, taps keys like a programmer, making the phone beep and vibrate. "Hey, all his numbers are prime."

"What?"

"Prime. Can't be divided. Three, five, seven." Patronizing: "Now, I'm making the phone call itself. If there's a wiretap—" Busy signal honks from the tiny phone. "No, see, it's clean—"

"Where did you—"

"Internet. Heard of it?"

Someone has ripped the pay phone out of its mount. Someone else has engraved DAPHNE BITES in the glass of the booth.

"How come you never told me you were an actor?" Rachel asks, giving him the phone back.

"What?"

"Are you embarrassed because you're not famous?"

"Maybe being famous isn't the point."

"Doh."

"It's just a job I do."

"Yeah, right. Busted. You're totally embarrassed. That's why you didn't mention it until the little beyotches showed up and got all totally stupid about it. And, BTW? I don't actually get what you're doing, Jack. Running away? No, that's what I'm doing. Aren't you supposed to be trying to prove you didn't kill her?"

"You don't know what you're talking about."

"You only run away if you did it, dork."

"Okay, look, this is the end of the line for you, little sister," Jack says to her. "Reach for the rip cord—figure out who we're gonna call when I'm done here, because I am not taking care of you anymore."

"Oh. Is that what you're doing?"

"Yeah. Pretty much."

"Cuz," Rachel drawls for effect, "it would appear otherwise, and I'm not counting on it."

They stare at each other coldly. Then Rachel says, "I saw the way you looked at her. When she walked into the restaurant. You have to go back."

"Saw the way I looked at who?"

Rachel just waits for him to catch up.

"Or whom. Who or whom, I can never fucking tell."

Rachel just waits.

"You don't know what you're talking about," Jack re-observes.

"You didn't kill her. You wouldn't hurt her. You have to go back and prove it."

"Prove it."

"What is wrong with you?"

A milk-beige pickup rumbles into the parking lot and circles the Sunbird, where Hudson and Brandee are still at war. Jack stalls, deciding what and who to dial. Rachel stares at him disappointedly, then out at the parking lot. Jack keys a number and presses Talk. He can hear the call go through, and a phone rings on the other end.

In the big bedroom of her house in the Hope Ranch hills of west Santa Barbara, Hannah, Jack's surgically near-perfect and silico-pneumatic ex-paramour lies, Rubenesque: naked, blonde and pale and languid, beneath a stark, valentine-red comforter and sheets.

A Lufthansa courtesy sleep mask covers her eyes. The ringing phone has awakened her. Hannah pushes the mask off, and reaches for the bedside portable, exposing a wild crisscross of stitches over a slender, bruised-purple, horizontal wound that spans her wrist like half a bracelet. She tugs off a fat pearl earring and presses the receiver to her ear.

Hannah says, "Hello?"

No one responds. She can hear traffic, though, very distant. And people arguing. A rattle of glass and metal. A shifting of weight. And wind.

"Hello?"

There is emptiness on the line, less than nothing. But Hannah waits.

Jack folds the phone gently to hang up.

"Who was that, who'd you call?"

Jack looks at Rachel. "Your turn."

"Call somebody else. C'mon, Jack. What are you doing?"

Jack holds out the phone.

"No. No," she repeats, "I won't go back unless you do."

Jack sighs. "I only knew her for one day," he explains.

Rachel shrugs. "So? In seventh grade I went steady with this boy for four hours. But, it was, like, the most incredibly intense relationship of my whole life." And letting the phone-booth door spring shut, Rachel walks away.

The stocky driver of the beige truck is out from behind the wheel, pale, sweating, doubled up. It's Symes, and he leaves the door open. "You assholes are in so much trouble," he barks at Hudson and Miller, who look like little kids caught shoplifting, and start moving dutifully toward him, mouths slack, heads down, shamefaced.

"Did you think I wouldn't find out? You think you're the first lazy fucktards who tried to short sheet a survival week? Christ almighty! How you gonna survive in the sandbox? Huh? I'm not gonna be there to fucking remind you to shit or shoot." Symes looks kind of green. He clenches his teeth and shudders. "I put a fucking GPS locator in your hump bags, I knew what you were planning before you even planned it."

And then he's moving, in a weird sort of half crouch, toward the café. "Do not move. Do not breathe. I gotta hit the can. And then we'll discuss what to do with you pieces of shit."

"Curse of the Big Sipper," Miller mumbles, under his breath.

"I heard that!" Symes says. He pushes through the side door of the restaurant and the glass shimmers, erasing him as he hustles toward the men's room.

Growing up in Chula Vista, Hudson had developed certain iron-clad rules about fast food, including (1) never order the ham at Arby's, (2) never eat an Oki Dog after midnight, and never, ever eat two, (3) never special order during peak hours because the kitchen help will spit in your McChicken sandwich, (4) you will eat the meat of a small pet, or squirrel, in at least one in twenty roach-coach meals, (5) avoid the fresh salads and seafood unless it's a salad bar or fish place, (6) popcorn shrimp isn't seafood, (7) curly fries are always a disappointment. So when he sees the Styrofoam bowl of what looks to be chopped tomato, onion, cilantro, and fish byproducts tilted on the passenger's seat of Symes' truck, and the half-finished Dr. Pepper in the cup holder, and the untouched bag of tortilla chips, Hudson deduces with some confidence the source of the old gunnery sergeant's gastric misfortune.

"Is that ceviche?" Miller has forgotten Brandee and her rage and disappointment. She and Vicko are in conference at the red convertible, but they might as well be in San Diego already.

Hudson winces. "Dude."

The parking lot, so dead just a moment ago, is alive with movement. First it was the trolling beige pickup disgorging a hunched-over hard body who screamed at the grunts, and now, as Jack tries to catch up with Rachel and give Hudson's phone back, a familiar khaki Cherokee with Border Patrol decals cuts him off, and the sunburned INS agent is leaning out at him. "Hey."

Jack acknowledges him, busted, mouth dry. Smiles, and keeps walking, trying to cut back behind the Jeep.

"Wait." Jack stops. The agent puts the Cherokee in reverse and rolls back to him. He's studying Jack, intent: "Where do I know you from?"

Jack reads the look, relaxes; it's a look he understands. "Television?"

The INS agent just stares, mouth half open to speak, eyes fixed on something he's on the verge of remembering. Rachel comes around the front of the car, worry on her face. Jack tries to look her off with his eyes, but she's determined to run interference.

"Whoa. Homeland Security," she says snottily, "keeping us safe from dark people and WMDs."

"Fuck off," the agent tells her. And then he has it: "*Star Trek: The Next Generation*! Helmsman with the nanovirus."

Jack grins. "Got me."

Rachel opens her mouth, and then closes it again.

"You tried to blow up the ship."

"I failed."

"Yeah, but—" The agent bares his teeth, a nonsmile one smiles in the presence of the semi-famous. "Oh boy, but you got close, didn't you?"

The agent makes a gun with his hand and fires it at Jack, winking. Then he throws a dark look at Rachel, puts the Jeep in gear, and powers toward the street.

The helmsman-with-the-virus feels his pulse skip a beat, then starts to walk toward the marines, steady and slow. He wiggles tingling fingers and breathes air fouled with garbage and gasoline cooked by the obdurate sun.

"You were on *Star Trek*?" Rachel dogs him.

"Let's get out of here," Jack says.

"This is fucked six ways to Sunday," Hudson observes gloomily.

"You know, it's not that I can't commit," Miller is arguing to Hudson, who doesn't care, but Miller's merely trying to rationalize himself, to himself. "God and country," Miller says. "I put my pale butt on the line for democracy and freedom and a war to win." Miller smacks his hands together, "To the limit, man. Totally and truly to the limit."

"We're taking off," Jack says, joining them. He holds out the cell phone. "Thanks."

But Hudson distractedly angles his head toward the café and calls out, "You all right, Sarge?"

Pale and unsteady, Symes walks shaky-serpentine into sunlight from the side door of the café, his short-sleeved plaid shirt deeply stained with half-moon pit sweat, his face flushed red, cheeks wet. He's been crying. Now Jack recognizes the stocky old marine and takes a wary step back.

"You look sick," Miller agrees, and makes a face at the Styrofoam bowl on the seat in the truck. "Sir, with all respect, you don't want to eat that noise."

At first, Symes doesn't see Jack. He just blinks, dizzy. He shifts his weight, hitching up his pants in a very career-military way. "Why not?" Symes asks, still reeling from his desultory campaign in the Gato Verde men's room.

Jack takes another step back, undone by Symes. He reaches for Rachel, but can't take his eyes away from the marine. Who finally locates him.

"Holy shit," Symes says. "You."

The sergeant lunges, Jack backpedals, Miller and Hudson are rooted in the open door of the truck. Jack pivots, turns to run, but Symes crashes down on him, muscle and motion, and Jack thinks: Mona was right, I'm no match for this guy.

They sprawl on the pavement. Jack is down, the side of his head is numb, Brandee and Vicko are screaming, Jack smells the dust and tastes the salt of his own blood. Strangely, though, Symes chooses this moment to float away, up and off of Jack. His weight becomes negligible; Jack has braced himself for blows that never come. It takes several dull-witted seconds for Jack to understand that the two jarheads, Hudson and Miller, have pulled Symes away from him. Symes is trying to make them understand, but he's light-headed and incoherent: "Killed her—killed her kids—guy's a, let me, he's a fucking butcher, he's a fucking. Butcher!"

Jack scrambles to his feet.

And runs.

Runs. Blood coursing in his ears, thump of his feet on the sidewalk, bite of Symes' screaming. He cuts between two discount pharmacies and into an alley, cowboy boots sloshing through puddles of what smells like raw sewage. A pack of scrawny dogs scatters, barking, then regroups to pursue (but with no actual desire to catch him).

Runs. Chain link and cinder block. Runs. Vacant prefab windows and rebar that juts skyward where walls just stop. A rotting sofa bed. A legion of rusting refrigerators chained together against a loading dock.

An engine guns, distant, tires squealing. Symes? The long alley spills out onto another empty sidewalk, and Jack jams through, cuts across sleepy traffic, leaving barking, honking, and storefront hip-hop in his wake, up a narrow concrete stairway between two warehouses bedizened with elaborate, spray-painted gang markings, and then into the shadow of a small stucco Christian church in the tiny courtyard of which is a crumbling, waterless fountain.

Jack disappears into the gloaming of a narrow passageway behind the chapel and stops, out of breath. Listening.

Alone. Exhausted. The squealing of tires around a corner gooses him again. Jack is too exhausted to run anymore. He tries the side doors of the church. They're open, quite heavy; he slips inside and then waits in a cramped corridor, letting his eyes adjust to the dim light. Catching his breath.

Through another, open doorway, the nave is all dusty, filtered dying light, and vacant. As if God's moved out. The few flickering candles, stuck fast to the railing of a kind of found-object chancel that may be a salvaged banister from a mid-seventies motel, cast deep shadows that throw into sharp relief the holes and cracks in the low wall behind the altar, where a huge cross has been removed, leaving only an outline, chased by time into the plaster. Jack walks the concrete floor between rows of folding chairs. He sits near the front, gazes up at the empty space where the cross once hung. Jack hasn't been to a church in more than twenty years.

A pastor emerges from a doorway. A young man, with fine

features framed by unruly hair pulled back in a ponytail secured
with a scrunchy. He looks like he's had too much coffee, too
much sun. He wears blue jeans, maroon flip-flops, and a tar-
black clergy shirt under a Chivas soccer jersey.

"*Usted necesita salvar?*" he asks in Spanish.

Jack looks up blankly. The pastor sees that he's Anglo, repeats
himself exactly, this time in flat, unaccented English:

"Do you need to be saved?"

Jack thinks about this for a moment. "No," he says. In fact, he
does, but adds, in case this clergyman thinks he does, "I'm just
resting. Is that okay?"

The pastor sits down in the pew in front of Jack. Jack wipes at
his eyes, self-conscious. The back of his hand comes away smeared
red with blood from his head wound, and Jack feels a need to
explain his intrusion even further, "The door was open,"—he
indicates the gash on his forehead vaguely—"I was . . . mugged.
Robbed. Gangsters. They took my wallet."

"Do you need a doctor?"

"I don't know."

"Can you walk?"

"I ran here. Yes."

The pastor smiles easily, already starting to stand up. He has
three gold caps on one side of his mouth. "Well, come on then."
He leads Jack through a small side door into a back room. Here,
boxes are stacked from floor to ceiling, forming a narrow canyon
that ends in the open doorway of another room, this one brightly
lit, a sort of clerical office cluttered with more half-packed ship-
ping boxes, and, in one corner, a couple dozen cases of California red table wine.

The pastor motions for Jack to sit in one of three wooden
chairs at a table covered with letters, bills, paperwork, two tele-
phones, and small, rusted tin boxes. He disappears, and then

returns almost immediately with a cheap plastic first-aid box he might have picked up at Walmart. He studies Jack's forehead wound for a moment before sorting through the supplies for an adequate remedy.

"Ah." Gauze, tape, a tiny bottle of hydrogen peroxide, some cotton swabs. "You'll have to self-medicate, I'm afraid."

"Excuse me?"

The man is already on his feet again, back to the cases of wine, not surprised to find one of the boxes open and a bottle inside with the cork already pulled. He brings this back and puts it on the table in front of Jack and removes the clean, folded handkerchief from his back pocket to dutifully wipe the bottle's rim. Gesturing for Jack to drink.

"A sister congregation in Ohio keeps sending us sacramental wine," the pastor explains, and dabs at Jack's cuts with a clod of cotton soaked in peroxide. "Charity for their immigrant brothers and sisters. I sell it on eBay."

Jack takes a swig of wine, and it burns going down like some kind of acid.

"'We do not need anymore wine,' I email them. Of course, it keeps coming. Christians are stubborn." He steps back to assess his repairs. "I am noticing your boots. They look quite expensive."

"I didn't buy them."

"Your eye," he says, pointing, "this one—"

"Blind. A childhood accident."

"Jesus weeps. It's a sign."

"No, the pupil just tore in a tear shape. It doesn't hurt or anything."

"Oh, good." Nods. "I mean, I'm sorry."

"Long time ago."

"'Better for thee to enter into life with one eye rather than having two eyes to be cast into hellfire.'"

"That sounds like it's from the Bible."

"You're not a Christian."

"My parents were Methodists. I remember going to a lot of Sunday school, coloring books with Jesus, hearing the story about him turning fish into loaves and wandering around the desert and the Sermon on the Mount. Mary. Moses, the Ark. That count?"

"It all counts," the pastor says. "Do you feel like taking Jesus into your heart right now, my friend?"

"No. Thanks, though," Jack adds.

"I see." The pastor has a nervous tic, something he does with the corner of his mouth, an aborted frown, or half a smile, upside down. "And was she pretty?" he asks pointedly. "This girl who makes you run through the streets and shadows to the arms of God?"

Jack thinks: Where did this come from? How does he know there's a girl? "Do you have a cigarette?"

"I don't." The pastor gestures for Jack to have more wine. "You were in love with her. Deeply, I think, señor. Your body aches with the love. But it is an earthly love. Your pores sweat the loss of it like an addict's."

"What kind of church is this?"

The pastor leans on the table, his face too close to Jack's after no sleep and too much red wine too fast. His breath thick and rich and sour with fermented California grapes, the pastor says, "It depends upon what you want."

"I want a phone," Jack says. "And a ride out of town."

"These are earthly wants. Jesus rose from the dead. Think about that."

Jack does consider it for a moment. "What do you want me to want?"

The young clergyman smiles. "Your problem is no problem. If Jesus can defeat death, your problems are nothing to him. He can do anything, he can help you do anything, you just have to accept him, you see? You just have to ask him. That's what kind of church this is. It's a church for people like you, people who are running away, people who are trying to forget.

"Do you think you can ask him?" the pastor says.

"Oh fuck," Jack says suddenly, his head spinning, light. "I forgot my sister."

When they return to the Gato Verde parking lot in the pastor's rusted Subaru wagon, the sun has just disappeared, leaving incredible, fiery ribbons in the sky. A slur of violent light. Contrails, Jack surmises, from commercial jet corridors to San Diego and Tijuana, or maybe Navy training flights, but it's beautiful, all the same.

"Rachel was the first and favorite wife of Jacob," the pastor observes.

In darkness, the Gato Verde looks like a different place, all hard shadows, café-turned-club, overflowing with young people and an overcranked pseudo-sambista band playing under the colored lights deep inside. A steely *repique de mao* makes the big glass windows shudder and heave.

Mona would want to dance, Jack thinks.

He has already considered the possibility that Symes has Rachel, and is waiting for him. But Symes doesn't know about Rachel running away with Jack, or what she might mean to him, and by the time Hudson and Miller got it sorted out, Rachel would have been shrewd enough to make herself disappear. He's hoping, however, that she somehow circled back here so that Jack could find her again, and he knows that it's a long shot.

Maybe this is where the Jesus thing kicks in, Jack thinks, and I become Born Again.

The parking lot smells of cigarettes and discouragement under a vacant sweep of sky, and the pastor gets into an argument with a fat man in a wifebeater who appears to be charging to tell you where you can't leave your car. There are a lot of underage boys in shrunken black T-shirts smoking cigarettes outside the front door, and nobody who looks remotely like Rachel.

"She's not here," Jack says, discouraged.

"Perhaps she went looking for you," the priest suggests. "Perhaps she didn't believe you'd come back."

Jack hangs back while the pastor talks to some of the smoking boys in a kind of Spanglish that seems completely made up. Panic is pressing down on him; he's trying not to get too far ahead of himself with dark speculation about what has happened to the girl. Inside, the sambista band's *repinique* rattles like a snake.

Suddenly the pastor gets very excited and everyone gets quiet and their faces turn to Jack expectantly, and the priest says, "She was here. And this boy saw your sister go across the street with El Tejón."

"What? Go where?"

"Across the street." The boy has a steel rod pierced through his eyebrow, full braces, and a couple of tear tattoos.

The pastor starts to pull Jack to the sidewalk. "A pimp," he says simply.

"A what?" Jack thinks he must have misheard.

"He is probably called The Badger because of the hair on his body, I don't know."

"A pimp?"

"Yes. El Tejón. The Badger."

"Shit."

"Yes."

A stillborn, suffocating heat has settled out of the night. There is a dream that Jack has occasionally. In it he's somehow caused the death of someone he doesn't know. This always happens before the dream starts, so it's also not entirely clear whether it was intentional or not, but there is guilt, and there is fear. But after a short period of panic, during which Jack wrestles with the morality of concealing and getting away with what he's done, Jack becomes fully aware, in his dream, that he's dreaming, that none of it has happened, that he won't ever have to face the consequences of what he's done. And the dream always sustains, long enough to allow Jack the exhilarating sensation of vindication and relief. He wants this to be a lucid dream. He wants to wake up, halfway, and discover that he's blameless.

The priest crosses the street ahead of Jack, and disappears into the neon-framed doorway of a *caja de la fortuna*. Fortune-teller. A big-ass half-ton slams on its brakes and redistributes its load of concrete block, the driver honking and yelling at Jack to get the hell out of the way.

Then Jack is in front of the fortune-teller's open door. The bent neon hums and rattles, and a beaded curtain trembles and sways just inside, where voices are raised, and Jack hesitates, fearing the worst, heart hammering, imagining a tiny room beyond, where gothic sconces bleed feeble piss-colored light and a gnarled wood table covered in purple sateen holds an actual crystal ball; where a cushioned chair is overturned and there are shelves stacked with talismans, fetishes, balms, and remedies, and where smoke from a switch of incense coils crooked and gathers into haze that wreathes the raw features of a snarling proprietress locked in argument with the pastor. Where is the girl? *No sé,* the psychic keeps spitting back at him.

No sé, no sé. A fat, shirtless pimp reels out of the shadows with Rachel locked in his arm, and the pastor has a gun, a handgun, and he's shoved the barrel into the keening fortune-teller's ear as he shouts at her to answer to God and Jesus and tell the pimp to release the girl. The terrified woman swoons to her knees, her eyes rolling back; she's weeping, pleading, praying, her hands clutching at the pastor's jeans as El Tejón lurches and Rachel struggles to breathe. Everyone is screaming, and the Marine Hymn is playing, distant, and nothing in Jack's life has prepared him for this and he keeps thinking, What have I done? What the fuck have I done?

But only a moment after his hesitation, Jack has slipped through the beaded curtain, and he's standing in a modest, largely empty whitewashed storefront with patterned linoleum flooring and a sagging red love seat facing some folding chairs. The fortune-teller is large and round and soft and smiling and reclining on the ruby sofa, her paisley muumuu nested under wildly painted toes, and there's no argument, just cordial questions and murmured answers. And then someone untangles himself from the back room curtain and stumbles out, drunk. *Mi esposa,* he cries, plaintive and drunk. *No lastime a mi esposa!* He's tiny, balding, his feet are bare and calloused, and he wears a grease-smeared University of Wisconsin T-shirt. The fortune-teller waves him away.

Wisconsin.

The Badgers, Jack remembers.

The University of Wisconsin Badgers.

"Is that your phone ringing?" the pastor asks.

Jack feels in his pocket and finds Hudson's cell phone where he put it when he ran away from Symes. The display is lit, and the phone trembles and bleats its Marine Hymn ring tone.

Jack turns away, unfolds it, answering.

"Hello?"

Across the street, above the café and two blocks past it, the big marquee of a motor hotel flashes brightly: MILAGRO MILAGRO MILAGRO.

It's Rachel. "Jack? It's me." She sounds small, and angry, and just a little scared. "Where are you?"

thirteen

■

"So. You left the woman, the one that makes your heart cry, you left this woman and you feel guilty about it," the pastor is summarizing. "You confuse this with love," he laments.

The bus station where Rachel is waiting is wedged between a secondhand store and a tattoo parlor on First Street. The lobby is small, with a ticket counter and a couple of plastic benches along one wall.

"Love is selfless," the pastor says, after they've parked and spilled from the car. "It wants and asks nothing. Requires nothing, most certainly not your guilt. Guilt is a kind of deferred payment plan, like, say, a mortgage on real commitment, back when such a thing meant something. Love is elusive, cash is king."

He stops suddenly at the window of the secondhand store and presses his nose to the glass to examine a small carving, a santo—saint—with mournful eyes and blood painted on its hands and feet. "*El Señor de la Misericordia*. Oaxacan, I would venture to guess. Wood, gesso, paint, hollow sound when knocked; closed eyes, no lashes, wig. Rope crown. Fabric loincloth probably provided by a pious local *benefactora* who clipped it from the hem of her finest *vestido*." He looks at Jack. "Tucson, Santa Fe, you could sell an item like this for five hundred American dollars, or more."

"I don't have any money," Jack says.

"Love is elusive, cash is king. They accept credit, though."

Rachel is standing in front of the bus station, arms folded, looking older than her fourteen years. She sees Jack, doesn't smile, but starts walking purposefully toward them.

"In Los Angeles, I had a crisis," Jack admits to the pastor in a rush. "Or, more like, I caused this crisis, and I ran from it, to the high desert, and fell into the arms and comfort of a woman I thought would be, you know—"

"Your *absolución*."

"What?"

"Salvation."

"No. Maybe. Whatever." Jack takes a moment, remembering. "But it became something else. And I flinched."

"Flinched?"

"Blinked. It was too bright, I blinked. And when my eyes opened again it was, it had already turned into, something else. Something ugly that the police think I did." Jack studies the scruffy clergyman for judgment, finds none in the steady, slightly impatient gaze.

"The high desert is a cruel landscape."

"Yeah."

"'The Spirit itself beareth witness with our spirit, that we are the children of God.' Romans 8:16."

"Okay," Jack says.

"There's this really sketchy guy in there," Rachel interjects, arriving, gesturing back to the storefront station. "I think he took a dump in his pants, and is afraid to stand up."

"Anyway. So, again, I ran," Jack finishes. "I ran away from her and I ran away from the problem and that's how I wound up in your church."

A pause. The pastor looks at Rachel. "Hello."

"Hi."

"I keep running away from things," Jack adds unnecessarily, and realizes, to his discomfort, that this is a confession, and neither he nor the pastor is Catholic.

"There are no solutions here," the cleric says finally.

"There are no solutions here," Jack agrees.

As Jack suspected, Rachel had removed herself from the psychodrama of Symes and the marines and the parking lot in the chaos of the moment following Jack's escape. Symes had hopped in his truck and zoomed up and down adjacent streets trying to find Jack. Vicko and Brandee got in the Sunbird, destined for San Diego, leaving their boyfriends to fend for themselves. Rachel hid in the broken phone booth, crouched down where they couldn't see her, not that they were actively looking. After a few minutes, Hudson and Miller hoisted their backpacks and set out on foot for the border crossing. She could hear them arguing about what happened for more than a couple of blocks. Then she wandered around Calexico for what seemed like hours, until she found the bus station and convinced the ticket seller to let her use their office phone.

"I remembered your number," Rachel says, "because of all the primes. Which in no way means I'm good at math, FYI," she adds defensively. "I don't care what Mr. Dickweed Davis says."

The pastor asks Rachel if she's accepted Jesus as her God and savior and Rachel says, politely, no, no not yet, and looks at Jack for some explanation, but, getting nothing, informs them that there's a bus to Anaheim that arrives a little after midnight.

"How will you pay for it?" asks the pastor.

"If you could find it in your heart to loan us the money, Father, I'd pay you back. I could wire the money back. I could wire double the money you loan us back."

"I'm nobody's father," says the pastor irritably. "And why would I do this?"

"It's the Christian thing, isn't it?"

"How would you know?"

Jack shifts, uncomfortable, exposed. "Look, what do you want—me to beg? Okay, yeah, I'm begging you. Please."

"You're not," the pastor says disparagingly. "You're whining. Begging requires commitment."

"I only have one eye," Jack says defensively.

"'If thine eye offend thee, pluck it out and cast it from thee! For it is better for thee to enter into life with one eye, rather than having two eyes to be cast into hellfire!'"

Jack says nothing for a long time.

"Matthew rocks," says the priest, smiling.

"It's fifty-nine dollars and twenty cents," Rachel tells Jack. "For ninety-nine dollars we can go anywhere in the United States."

Jack looks emptily down the street. He feels a cold discouragement. They'll probably catch him. He still has no plan.

"I have to go back," he tells Rachel.

"I know," she says. "I was just saying."

"You understand about Christ on the cross?" the pastor wonders. "The sacrifice He made for our safe passage to the other side?"

"What size are your feet?" Jack asks him.

fourteen

■

Jillian's home phone rings like a regular phone, which is annoying since sometimes she forgets what it is, and lets it ring longer than she should.

That's what's happened, because now the phone is ringing and there's steam on the mirror and the water is running in the basin and Jillian, slim, striking, thirtyish, an actress who hopes she's still in her prime, blinks back at herself through the mist, dark-eyed, no makeup, trying to decide whether her eyebrows are growing closer together and if it's the light that's too harsh or her face that's getting hard. Her terrycloth robe is unhooked in front, her red hair wet from the shower and combed back. The mirror tells no lies.

And the phone keeps ringing. Her landline. Jill's BlackBerry has a Gnarls Barkley ring tone, and she usually picks up before it even gets to the second measure because she hates Gnarls Barkley, which is the point.

But the classic ring of a landline is easily dismissed.

Reaching to the switch plate, she kills the lights, stares at the half-erased Jillian looking back, and then puts the lights back on again. Definitely the lights.

Jillian pulls out a drawer crammed full of beauty aids, finds a cordless Lady Schick electric razor, and lifts one long leg onto the counter, baring it. Grimaces, feeling the grit of hair stubble on her shin.

"You heifer," she says, to her reflection.

An ancient answering machine (are she and Jack the only two people on earth who still have them?) picks up—"Hi, this is Jillian. Leave a message. I'll get back to you when I get back"—as Jillian simultaneously discovers that her Lady Schick is broken. She shakes it, as if that will help. Throws it back into the drawer and begins searching the vanity under her sink as the message machine beeps, distantly, and she hears:

"Sir, there is no answer."

"She's in there," Jack's voice, "if we can just—Jillian?"

"Sir, you're going to have to—"

"—it's me, Jilly, pick up!"

"—call back another time—"

Jillian gropes under the clothing clumped on the bathroom floor, finds the cordless phone receiver and answers, "I'm here, I'm here."

"Will you accept charges?"

"Jack?"

"Yeah."

"Ma'am, I need you to—"

"I'll accept the call, yes."

"Go ahead, sir."

The message machine doesn't turn off, so Jillian hears Jack's voice eerily echoing from the other room, and her own voice doubled. She sort of likes it, the approximate vocal experience of looking at herself in a window reflection as she walks past.

"Jack, where are you?"

"Calexico."

From way, way back in the cabinet, Jillian retrieves a can of Barbasol aromatic shaving cream that has a disposable razor rubber-banded to it.

"Listen, Jilly, I gotta get on a bus here momentarily, so," Jack is saying, "favor time—"

"As if there were any other time, with you," Jillian says, letting foam ooze from the nozzle of the shaving cream can. "What bus?" And then, "Is this your shaver and shaving cream under my sink?"

"Probably. I used to hide it, so you wouldn't wreck my razor clear-cutting your calves."

Jillian cradles the receiver against her shoulder, folds back her bathrobe, and begins to spread the shaving cream on her right leg.

"Has anyone called you about me?" Jack asks. "Is anyone up there . . . looking for me or anything?"

"You mean like Spielberg or somebody? Gee, I don't think so, Jack. Not this week."

"Ha ha."

"Only your agent. I wish you'd inform him that you put me in turnaround, baby. He's always calling here. It's pretty depressing, sometimes, actually."

The razor tickles her skin. It's a sharp one, so she doesn't press too hard.

"Oh, and Tory," Jillian adds, remembering. "Tory was looking for you. But it didn't sound urgent, it was more, I don't know, metaphysical. I mean, it's Tory, so. Where are you?"

"Calexico. My agent called?"

Jillian picks up the razor. Starts to shave her leg. "Calexico."

"Yeah."

"As if I'm supposed to know where that is."

Something rumbles past on Jack's end, garbling his reply. "What?"

"What?"

"No, you—what?"

"I said I've got to get on the bus, now."

"What bus?"

The sliding razor feels good on Jillian's skin. Sharp and sinfully uncomfortable.

"Are you working today, Jilly?" Jack asks tentatively.

fifteen

■

The Twentynine Palms police station wagon follows a Santa Monica Police Department patrol sedan to the tree-lined curb in front of a vintage, two-story duplex. Soles and Ng get out of the wagon, stretching their stiff legs. The neighborhood is quiet. An overweight SMPD uniformed cop struggles out of his car, and they all cross the driveway, climb concrete stairs to the upper unit.

The local cop is breathing hard. Ng rings the bell. Knocks. Then pries open the door with a screwdriver.

"So this is a bad search, now," the Santa Monica cop tells them.

"Don't care," Soles tells him.

"You got no warrant."

Ng sneezes. "Smog. I'm allergic."

"No smog out here," the cop says. Ng and Soles share a look. "I'm serious, it all blows inland."

The door swings open. Soles and Ng enter first. The fat cop

hangs back, pretty disinterested. "If we did something like this," he says, "brass'd kick my keester to traffic duty and back again. You got no warrant."

Soles picks up a big envelope somebody slid under the door, while Ng studies the main room. The place is trashed. Furniture overturned, bookshelves emptied and splintered, pictures shattered.

Soles turns to the cop. "You want to go downstairs and ask the neighbors if they heard this? Saw anything?"

"No." He stares back stubbornly. Soles decides not to press it. Ng has disappeared. "Anything you find in here. Inadmissible," the cop lectures him. Soles looks closely at the big envelope. It has "Warner Bros.—By Messenger—Direct" scrawled on it in secretarial block letters. He rips it open, and pulls out three green script pages.

"You guys are unbelievable," the fat cop says.

Across the top of the script page "Father Zorn" is scrawled in a different handwriting from the envelope.

"Sides," says the fat cop. Soles frowns. "For an audition. Actors get sent a scene to try out for a part, they call 'em sides. Don't ask me why. My brother-in-law's a gaffer, that's how I know about it."

Soles wants to know what a gaffer is, but debates the wisdom of encouraging more chitchat with this guy.

"Hey," the cop says. "Long board." He picks up Jack's surfboard and leans it against the wall. "This is worth something."

Ng is in the kitchen, not touching anything. Solving a puzzle. The refrigerator door is open. Food is scattered everywhere— it looks like some of it has been violently thrown at the walls. What is this all about? Glassware and dishes, smashed. The phone machine broken into pieces.

"He's mad at himself," Ng proposes to himself, aloud. It sounds wrong as he says it. You don't ransack your own house.

Cat food by the back door.

A full bowl, hardly touched.

Soles comes in, still carrying the script sides. "Bedroom's same. Mattress slashed. Our Jack's having one crappy week."

"Where's the cat?" Ng asks.

"I wish there were more of us," Soles says, following his partner out of the kitchen and back down the hallway. Ng ducks into the bathroom, turns on the light, and doesn't come out. Soles hears the sound of the toilet running continuously. He calls out to the waiting Santa Monica cop.

"Any chance we could get one of your forensics units out here to give us a hand?"

"What's the point?"

"What?"

"What's the point. You got no warrant. It's a bad search."

"We're trying to figure out where he is," Soles says. "We know what he's done. And this is not where he did it." He waits for the answer to his question.

The Santa Monica cop sighs. "Do you know how many folks die or disappear every day in this city?" He smiles condescendingly. "Forensics. Sure. Maybe next year, brother."

Ng calls out from the bathroom, "Found him."

Through the bathroom doorway, Soles can see a slice of Ng staring into the toilet.

"What's he talking about," the fat cop says, coming into the hallway, from the living room.

"Baylor?" Soles asks, knowing he must be wrong.

"No, the cat." Ng comes to the bathroom doorway. "Drowned. Not an accident."

sixteen

■

"I swear, you are so lucky."

Traffic jam on the 405. Pack-a-snack. Even at 1:00 AM. Unbelievable. Miles of aisles of glutinous metal, glass, and rubber.

"It's like, okay, so yesterday I'm on set eighteen hours, which means of course they don't want to force my call today—but tomorrow? 5:30 pickup." Jillian shakes the hair out of her eyes, "And here I am driving at midnight to Anaheim to rescue you and your jailbait from another Jack Baylor special."

From the backseat: "Who's jailbait?"

Jillian pretends she didn't hear. "You owe me."

The smoggy nightglow does magic with Jillian's delicate features. She looks great. Lipstick, eye shadow, and hair products are, Jack knows, her best friends, and here, now, in her car on the San Diego Freeway crawling north through the spackle of city lights, they work together to lend her the kind of preternatural glow she obsessively craves.

Jack couldn't sleep on the bus, and is dead tired.

"I should have known when they sent the script over."

From the backseat: "I'm not jailbait."

"What script? Who?"

"Whatshisname. Your agent."

"Sent a script?"

"When he can't track you down he sends your shit to me. Sides, scripts, callback messages. You should tell him that we're not, well, you know. But I guess I don't mind."

Jack knows enough to say nothing, here.

"How do you do it, Jack? It's been what, less than a week since Hannah? And she was, oh, about the next day after me, as I remember it." Jillian frowns. "How many days between me and Annie?"

"You greatly exaggerate."

"I'm just saying."

"Do you have a cigarette?"

Jillian glances in the rearview mirror at Rachel. "Are you in on this, should we count you?"

"No."

"Cigarette, Jill."

"Maybe in the glove box. I've quit. Open the window, too."

Jack searches Jillian's overstuffed glove compartment, finds a crumpled pack of Virginia Slims with one and a half cigarettes left.

"Maybe you're sick, or something. Like an alcoholic. Maybe there's a group you could go to. 'Hi, my name is Jack. I'm a serial shithead.'"

"He is not," Rachel says.

Jillian flicks her gaze in the rearview. "Excuse me?"

"Maybe you guys just didn't have it."

"Awww. The kitty with claws," Jillian says to Jack. "Precious. But dangerous territory for you. Statutory, in fact."

"Leave her alone, Jill, huh?" Jack pushes the cigarette lighter in.

"Where are your boots? Since when are you a flip-flop guy?" Jack pretends he didn't hear her.

From the backseat: "I want a cigarette."

Jack ignores it.

"Are you in love with Mr. Terrific, sweetie?" Jillian asks Rachel.

"Shut up."

"He makes a good first impression, I can't argue with that."

"How old are *you*?" Rachel asks, as if innocently. Jillian is silent because the question cuts deep. Rachel folds her arms and stares out the window, putting her sneakers up on the back of the seat.

"Were you in love with me?" Jack asks Jillian. She looks at him.

"God, no."

Jack rolls his shoulders. The lighter pops out, and he presses it to the end of his cigarette.

"Put down the window."

Jack does. Jillian glances in the rearview at Rachel again, frowning. "What kind of question is that, Jack, was I in love with you?"

The traffic crawls along. Chrome glinting, headlights and tail-lights alive. For a long time, no one says anything. The draft sucks at Jack's open window, causing the inside of the car to flutter-boom like a blown bass speaker.

Finally he closes it, and the quiet seems like silence.

"You weren't in love with me, were you?" Jillian genuinely wonders.

The silverfish moon smolders through the usual marine layer, painting faintly the pale faces of bungalows and apartments on

Jack's tree-lined neighborhood street. Jillian's Audi slows and stops. Jack looks out at the dark, upper-floor windows of his duplex. Rachel starts to put her shoes back on.

"Who's taking care of Murphy?" Jillian asks.

"I left him a ton of cat food and two clean litter boxes."

"Are we getting out here?" Rachel says to Jack.

Jillian frowns at Jack, motionless beside her, just staring out at his home. "What."

"I don't have my keys," Jack says.

"Jesus, Jack, did she get your testicles, too?"

"I'm afraid to check."

"Um. What are we doing?" Rachel asks again, wanting mostly to put immediate, considerable distance between herself and the bitch Jillian.

"Yes, I've still got my key," Jillian says, thinking she's reading Jack's expression. She works to take it off her key ring. Jack glances up at the dark windows, frowning, wondering if they've traced him this far, if they're waiting up in the apartment for him.

"I can never work these things," Jillian says, wrestling with the key ring.

Jack looks up the street. He pulls the sun visor down and checks behind them in the vanity mirror.

Jillian holds out her key. "More serendipity. You're the king of helpful happenstance."

Jack doesn't take it. Headlights hit them suddenly, from a car coming down the street. In the visor mirror he sees a second car turning onto the street behind them.

"Drive away," he says, trying not to scare Jillian.

"What?"

"Jack—" Rachel starts to ask something, stops.

"Drive away!" Jack doesn't think he's shouting, but he makes Jillian jump. "Now!"

Jillian freezes. Jack moves his foot, jams it down onto hers, punching the accelerator, causing her Audi to swerve wildly out from the curb. The approaching sedan honks. Jillian struggles to regain control, barely avoids creasing the side door of the oncoming sedan, and the car's driver, another woman, screams an ugly obscenity at them as they slalom past her.

"Shit, Jack—"

Heart pounding, Jack glances in the visor mirror. The car behind has turned into a driveway.

"What is wrong with you?" But Jillian keeps driving away. Brake lights flaring at the next intersection, she turns the corner and the night is hushed again, the street empty, and Jack's duplex windows inscrutably dark.

Later, while Jack is opening up the sofa bed in the living room of her Fountain Avenue courtyard walk-up, Jillian comes in, robe, no makeup, carrying a big pair of men's cow-print pajama pants, sheets, pillow, and a pink, very girly comforter. A multicolored shooting script falls to the floor from the top of the linens and lands with a slap.

Jack wants to recognize the pajamas. "I don't remember leaving those here."

"They aren't yours."

Jillian starts to make the sofa bed. Jack wants to help, but has never quite figured out how to offer, and can't make a bed anyway, so, self-consciously, he gathers up the pajamas.

"Flannel," Jack says. "A sturdy, sensible guy, with just a skosh of whimsy. Real estate?"

Jillian shoots him a cold, indifferent look. She knows everything now, and Jack is pretty sure she believes him. Of course, she doesn't have much of a choice; if he actually did what the

Twentynine Palms cops say he did, Jillian would have to figure out what it means in the wide circle of her own life, and Jack knows her well enough to understand that she won't be too keen on opening that can of worms anytime soon. Still, it's awkward, Jillian knowing; another gut punch to the belly of Jack's rapidly deflating ego.

Rachel comes out of the bathroom, hair wet from a shower, wearing sweat clothes too big for her (Jillian's) and eating Wheat Thins from a box. "You guys want to watch *Adult Swim*?"

Blank stares tell her she's found a possibly useful generational wormhole.

"Cartoon Network," she explains. "It's—"

"Jack says you're running away from home," Jillian interrupts.

"Mmm hmm." Rachel looks at Jack, then Jillian. Puts down her Wheat Thins and takes up a sheet corner to help finish making the bed. Just like that, Jack thinks. You don't offer, you just do it.

"How old are you?"

Rachel stuffs the sheet under the stiff wafer of sofa bed mattressette.

"Do you live in Los Angeles?"

"Are you asking because you're interested? Or because you think, I dunno, what you should do is ask?"

Jillian lets Rachel finish making the bed, and for a moment just stands there, arms folded, looking at Jack. "Let's suppose I'm interested," she says.

"Well, it's none of your fucking business," Rachel says.

Jack goes into the bathroom and closes the door. Rachel hops on the bed, finds the TV remote on the side table and starts to channel surf.

"Do you have a plan? For running away, I mean," Jillian asks her.

"I'm running. Away. That's the plan."

"Relatives you can go to, or friends, or, um—"

"Huh. Um." Rachel's not listening.

Jillian sits down on the edge of the bed. "You can't hang with Jack, Rachel. It's . . . it could be construed to be, you know, illegal. You'll get him in a lot of trouble."

Rachel regards Jillian blankly. "Oh." A pregnant pause. "More trouble than he's in?"

"It doesn't matter what you actually do," Jillian presses. "You're underage. He's—"

"—not your boyfriend anymore, so duh."

"Jesus, will you just—stop—"

"—acting my age? Fourteen? How old are you?"

"Fine."

Rhetorical this time: "How old are you?"

Jack comes out of the bathroom wearing the PJs. "Is that my toothbrush in the medicine cabinet?" Jillian and Rachel both glare at him.

"What?"

Nothing.

"Listen, Jillian, maybe this isn't such a good—I should get out of here, and—"

Jillian just cuts him off, breezy. "Hey. We're friends, Jack. I still care about you. Plus, now you owe me, big time, and I do intend, maybe when you least expect it, to collect." She plumps the pillow for Rachel's bed and drops it into place.

Jack notes the unused stack of sheets and blankets remaining. "What are these for?"

"The spare room. We'll have to rig up something for you on the floor. Since your ward is homesteading out here on Mr. Sofa Bed."

"Oh. I thought—" Actually, he assumed.

Jillian shakes her head, with a bittersweet smile. "Guy who belongs to those pajamas wouldn't understand."

"Got it." Jack smiles back, pro forma.

Rachel laughs at something on the TV. Jillian takes the remaining linens and crosses to the small spare room she uses as an extra closet. Stainless-steel rolling racks of her hanging clothes need to be pushed out of the way to make room for a square of carpet that will be Jack's bed.

"Have you talked to Hannah Banana?" Jillian unfurls a sheet in Jack's direction; he grabs the other end and becomes helpful.

"No. I tried."

"Tory?"

"Not yet."

They pull the sheet down, then another on top of it, and a couple blankets Jack will never use. Jillian looks for another pillow in the closet, where there are more clothes, and boxes, and a whole artificial Christmas tree, broken down into parts.

"You know that Hannah will tell him if I don't," Jack says.

"Fine. Let her."

"Maybe he already knows."

Jillian shakes her head. "He doesn't think you have the balls, Jack."

Jack sighs, looks out the door to Rachel, who seems pointedly trying to pretend she's paying attention to the TV, and not to their conversation. Jack lowers his voice. "I know what you think of him, Jill. He's my best friend. I need—"

"Right now you need money, you need clothes, and you need a ride out of town." Jillian is stuffing sweaters into a pillowcase. It will be lumpy, but soft. "You don't need Tory," she adds.

"I'm innocent," Jack says, hearing a calmness he doesn't feel. Am I acting? he wonders. "Sooner or later the police out there

are going to figure it out. I'll be able to come back. It will be better if Tory hears it from me."

"How? What can you possibly say? You fucked his wife, Jack!"

"He's my best friend."

"He's not! Listen to yourself! You know he's not!" Jillian
catches herself shouting, lowers her voice. "You grew up with
him, that's all. He's a greedy, manipulative, miserable, self-
important asshole who beats up on his trust-fund wife and you
tried to help her in the only way you know how."

This is so true Jack doesn't know what to say.

"He's some of that baggage you claim you don't carry
around," Jillian says.

They fall silent. This is where they were in their relationship
when Jack decided to punch out. Lots of empty silences. Rachel is
watching a show called *Full Metal Alchemist* in the other room.
There's an uproar of Japanese sound effects.

"Not everyone's going to be your best friend when you grow
up, hon. Not every decision you make's going to be the right
one. It piles up. Hannah, Tory. Me." Jillian stands up to leave
the room.

"How come we didn't work out, Jilly?"

"Oh, fuck, I don't know." She thinks about it. "Runners, Jack,"
she says after a while. "We're both runners."

"You hate running."

"Not that kind." She blinks a couple of times, as if her contact lenses went dry. "Running fast, in different directions. So."
And then she's all efficient again, organizing and making lists:
"Money. Clothes. Transportation. A long-term strategy. Stay
focused." Jillian walks out of the room and into her bedroom
and closes the door.

Jack lets the world go flat. If he relaxes, if he allows it, everything in front of him settles into one flat plane, a scrim that he

could theoretically just stroll around and get behind. Like walking off the set of a movie. There's Rachel, the television, the multicolored script on the floor behind the sofa. He walks out to get it; it has a clipped-on delivery label from a talent agency, Jack's name, care of Jillian. Rachel's program is an anime about a robot with a child's voice, a sloe-eyed boy with spastic hair, a cute girl with the big eyes and the high, sweet voice. If Rachel is aware that Jack's behind her, she doesn't turn around.

The script is 103 pages with pink, blue, yellow revisions, starred and numbered, a ghostly tracking number, and Jack's name printed diagonally across every page for security, as if it were a classified document, as if some nefarious enemy would want to get hold of it and, what? Read it? Show it to the Wrong People? Make a bootleg version of the movie? On the title page someone has hand-printed and circled in red Sharpie: ZORN.

Jack flips through it. Slowly at first, then faster. Page after page, looking for the character called Zorn.

There it is. Page seventy-six.

And part of page seventy-seven.

Two pages. One scene.

A referendum on Jack's career.

seventeen

■

Soft grey mist.

Dripping sounds.

"Yeah, Paul Pressman, please."

A towel wipes steam from a mirror, revealing Jillian's pink-and-black bathroom, always an eye-opener, Jack recalls. His shower-flushed face stares back at him, holding the portable phone receiver, two days growth of beard. The cut above his eye healing into a pink and purple mess.

"Hi Mindy, it's Jack Baylor. Is he in?" Jack listens to his agent's secretary recite the stall of the day while, he knows, she's sending a text message to Pressman's laptop to see if he wants to take Jack's call. "No," Jack answers to her idle question, "just out of town for a couple days."

Jack combs his hair straight back. A Bono look.

"Hey you," a voice raps, distorted, "you know why Pressman believes in a benevolent deity?"

"Paulie. You were looking for me?" Jack parts his hair in the middle, and stoops to look in the cabinet under the sink.

"Warners wants you for the Chung Wiley film."

"Can we talk about that name, for a sec?"

"No, Jack. You should have his fucking name, I don't care how stupid it sounds. Thank you. Thank you for making my day, I'd forgotten what a pleasure it is to talk to you. Asshole." All this said in a lively, friendly, conversational voice, no malice. Rooting through Jillian's health and beauty aids, Jack pictures his agent: a small, low-key man with a shaved head, suspenders, little loafers, and a pin-striped Wall Street suit, pacing the picture window of his Century City office. He wears a wireless headset that lends him a queer, impatient, magical elf quality.

"Jack? Is that, I'm hoping, the stunned silence of happy disbelief at getting a part in the new Wiley project, which people will kill their firstborn children to be a part of, or have you died on me?"

Jack finds what he was looking for: his shaving cream and razor. He doesn't see the fine, ladylike stubble stuck to the underside of the cartridge.

"I can't do it, I'm sorry."

"I'm sorry, I misheard you say you can't do it."

"I can't. I'm in kind of a bind."

"No, I'm still not hearing it right."

"Will you stop?"

"Jack, we're talking about a payday here. Major motion picture. That is your vocation."

Rachel opens the door suddenly, eyes gluey with sleep, and it bangs against Jack's head hard.

"Ow!"

"Oh, ohmygosh—sorry, Jack—"

"Jack?" Pressman's voice goes up half a key, curious.

"Yeah. Yeah, look." The door closes again. "I'm in kind of a bind, I actually need you to do me a favor." Jack stares at himself in the mirror, wondering if he gave that the proper timbre of urgency.

"Is this what the police called me about?"

"What police?"

"The police called. Two Bunch Palms. No. Or some place like that. Out in the desert, Palm Springsish. A Deputy Soles."

"Some speeding tickets I never paid."

"They wouldn't say what it was. Speeding tickets, ah, ha, right. Crafty bastards. I got nailed on the 210 transition. On the way to Vegas. In the M doing about 135. I told the cop I had family in law enforcement. Which. Technically. I do. Since all my cousins are lawyers. But he gave me the ticket anyway, now I'm doing the comedy traffic school, I got the instructor coming to my office. He thinks I can get him on Letterman."

Jack fills his hand with shaving cream and starts to lather his face. "I need you to advance me some money, Paul."

"They told me it was a felony investigation. Fuckers. Desert lawmen. Desperate for civic funds. Did I mention it's the new Chung Wiley film? What's the name of it? It used to be called *The Tourist*. Mindy, are you on, what's the name of it?" Pressman's assistant is always monitoring his conversations, presumably so he won't have to really listen to anything.

Jack hasn't moved. His razor hand is frozen inches from one cheek. It's trembling. He puts it down flat on the pink tile vanity counter, struggles to stay focused.

"*Loop the Loop*," Mindy is saying.

"*Loop the Loop*," Pressman says, as if Jack couldn't hear her. "I've read the script, it's fucking phat. Truly."

Phat. "What are you, something from an eighties surfer film?"

"Keanu Reeves," Pressman says laughing. "Cowabunga."

"I need you to advance me some money," Jack says again. "Doesn't Lorimar still owe me for that movie of the week?"

"Seriously. Part shoots today," Pressman says, as if he hasn't heard Jack at all. "Noon wardrobe call. You better get going."

Rachel's at the bathroom door again: "How long are you going to be in there, I've got to pee."

"Paul, listen, I'll swing by this morning for the cash, whatever you can spare. Tell the Chung Wiley people I'm really flattered but I don't have time to audition."

"Audition? No. And, footnote: as regards the former, I'm an agent, Jack, not a bank. Resuming: But you know what's good and wild? It's a firm offer. No audition. I already took this job for you. I said, 'Yes, Mr. Baylor would love to do this part for you.' I did it because you're a shameless whore, Jack, and I knew you wouldn't turn it down, and then I prayed, literally, that you'd check in with me. And here we are. Serendipity, Jack. See?"

"Jillian said that."

"I'm not kidding," Rachel says through the door.

Jack takes the phone, his razor and shaving cream, and a towel and opens the bathroom door. Rachel rushes past him, and the door slams shut behind her.

"Blindly now," Pressman says, regaining his momentum, "Pressman believes in his Yahweh. And? His Yahweh rewards him: you did call, you need this cash advance, it all lines up. Noon call. I'll send the money by courier to the set. See? Divine symmetry. When was the last time you went to a church, Jack?"

In the kitchen now, Jack just hangs up and puts down the phone. Noon call. A no-read offer on a shooting movie. Shit. There's no mirror, no one looking back at him. Jack runs water over his razor and then he starts to shave with a blade that has been pitted and ruined by a recent run across his old girlfriend's legs.

eighteen

■

"You don't have to do this," Jack says unnecessarily.

A man in cow-print pajama bottoms and a girl in a wrinkled sundress stand, gazing down a familiar, shady street at the row of Spanish-style apartments. They came by bus; Rachel opposite Jack, each of them on their own bench seat and Rachel pretending she didn't know him, because Jack's wearing Jillian's sunglasses, his shirt, the aforementioned pajama bottoms, a clergyman's flip-flops, and he's got little bits of toilet paper stuck to his face, where his razor has shredded his skin.

"It's okay." Rachel takes the apartment key from Jack, puts it into the pocket of her sundress.

"Now what?" Jack asks, when she doesn't move.

"Nothing."

"Nothing."

"I don't understand how you can go work on a movie when the cops are after you, and—"

"It's a no-read offer," Jack says, and thinks it explains every-thing.

"Oh." Rachel stares at him, frowning.

"Go in the back door. If you hear anyone come in—"

"Don't worry," Rachel says, and she darts across the street.

The key turns easily, but she has to wiggle the knob a bit to get it to open. For a moment she stands, listening. Careful.

"Hello?" No sound. No movement. "Murphy?"

Jack's apartment is a chocolate mess. For a moment, Rachel wonders if all grown-up single guys like to live in grungy squalor, or is it just Jack?

Then she understands. No, no: someone has searched the place.

Her movements are deliberate. Cat food is in the cabinet next to the dishwasher, a can opener in the second drawer down from the coffee maker, but there may be an already-opened can in the refrigerator. Rachel opens the fridge. Surprisingly tidy, and clean. There: Friskies flaked tuna, with a baggie rubber-banded over the top. Smelly food. Rachel makes a mental note to tell Jack that dry food is better, less fat, more protein, and no chance of urinary obstruction if your cat's been fixed, which it should be, these days; smelly cat food reminds Rachel, as she forks it into a plastic dish, of a newspaper story she read about two old ladies who were discovered living off cat food and dog biscuits they were buying with food stamps.

But even after the food is in the dish, and the can in the garbage, and the redolence of fish byproducts stinking up the kitchen, there's no sign of Murphy. Rachel, worried, looks for him, under the bed, under the sofa. Was he locked out? Is there an open window?

She backtracks in the hallway, lets her eyes get drawn to the photographs nailed there, mostly unframed, a brief Life History of Jack: acting jobs, Jillian, many other pretty women, a three-shot of Jack and some slick-looking guy and a breathtaking blonde in a wedding dress.

Rachel. Don't wander.

Top right bedroom bureau drawer, right-hand side, under an unused fanny pack, Rachel finds Jack's checkbook and a leather photo album with a few snapshots of a much younger Jack on a surfing trip to some island destination (Hawaii? Tahiti?), crammed together in front, none fixed to the never-filled pages. In the closet, she's startled by how many clothes and shoes Jack owns, then finds a pair of jeans and some Converse high-tops with white socks crammed inside.

Good, Rachel. One more thing and you're out of here.

Meanwhile, Jack, on the street corner in his bovine-motif jammies, watches helplessly while a dark-roots blonde with a sloppy-faced golden retriever comes charging up the street toward him, power walking in Jazzercise leggings and a VOTE FOR PEDRO T-shirt.

"Jack! Hey! I hear you got a gig!" She's talking to him when she gets within thirty yards. "The Wiley film. *Trust Me*? Snap. You must be so stoked."

Did she really say *snap*?

"I think it's called *Loop the Loop*."

A station wagon comes around the corner. Twentynine Palms Police emblazoned on both doors, a rack of unlit lights up top. Jack turns away, his chest tight and his fingers tingling.

"Yeah, um," he says to the blonde, whose name he can't remember, as she wrestles with the leash on her lunging, tongue-flailing dog. "Hunh."

The wagon double-parks in front of Jack's apartment. Ng and Soles get out. Jack crouches to pet the dog, and it nearly knocks him on his ass with its huge front paws. Sophie. Sophie is the dog's name.

"Hey, Sophie. Good girl."

"Sophia," the blonde says. "Not Sophie. Sophia."

Rachel doesn't hear the key turning in the front door because she's opening the big bottom drawer of the bathroom built-in vanity and finding a small cache of cash under a collection of airline complimentary shaving kits. Dislodged novelty nude-girl golf tees scatter across the floor, along with a fading, wallet-sized school photograph of a young boy in a gold-and-blue wind-breaker.

Jack at fourteen.

Rachel stares at the picture. Fourteen. Her exact age. She wonders if she would have talked to him; he looks, well, sketchy. Not particularly cute, or interesting. Then voices in the living room cause her head and eyes to pivot toward the open bathroom door.

"All he said was he didn't want us wasting our time on it anymore."

Soles' voice Rachel does not recognize, but she knows the other one, the deputy named Ng's: "Our free time."

"I mentioned that."

She reaches out and pushes the bathroom door halfway shut a moment before Soles and Ng walk past.

"So what're we supposed to do, just let this slide? Something fucked up happened. A woman and her kids are gone."

"Allegedly."

"Indisputably."

With gauzy footsteps Rachel crosses to the bathroom window, tries to open it. Stuck.

She turns away, panicky. And sees the cat drowned deep in the toilet. Looking up at her with nacreous eyes.

"—but they said that I was really really—Sophia, sit—*really* close and—good girl—it was just between me and this one other girl—"

Alice? Emma? Elizabeth? No. Jack watches the blank windows of his apartment, feeling anxious and helpless. Ella?

"—and what—Sophia, *sit*, sit, good girl—what it came down to was—"

Betsy.

"Betsy, I'm sorry—"

"—was they didn't want too many—"

"Betsy—"

"—you know—"

"I gotta go."

"—blondes in the cast. Sophia. What did I say, sweetie? Sophia, *sit*—"

Jack hurries down the street.

Soles dips his finger into the freshly served cat food. "Cold."

Ng hears him. Holds up an empty cat food can he's found on top of the trash under the kitchen sink. Shakes his head, staying silent. Together, as if synchronized, they look back down the hallway.

A moment later, they're at the bathroom door. Soles carefully noses it open with his service revolver, Ng behind him, gun drawn but held limp at his side, expecting nothing, inclines right to look just past Soles, into the bathroom—and sees a sliver of himself, tilting, reflected in the mirror above the sink.

Breathless from a half block of sprinting, Jack stands at the desert cops' station wagon, trying to think.

Trying to think.

A tiny red LED on the dashboard flashes in spasms. The light of a car alarm: cops can't be too careful, even out in the desert where bad things generally aren't supposed to happen.

Jack puts the palms of his hands flat on the hot front fender of the big car. Shoves once, tentatively, experimenting.

Nothing happens.

Soles goes into the bathroom first. As he does, Rachel slips out the side door that leads into Jack's bedroom, glancing back over her shoulder at Ng's gun, which precedes him as he, in turn, glides past Soles. They don't know about this second doorway into the bedroom, which is good news for Rachel, because while they're securing the bathroom, she sprints down the hallway toward the kitchen, fighting to hold back a typhoon of tears.

Soles hears Rachel's retreat on the hardwood floorboards, but as he starts to turn toward the sound a familiar car alarm starts wailing out on the street, he knows it's their car, and he lunges into the hallway to make the understandable mistake of looking first to the front door he left open, because if he turns the other way he'll see Rachel dart out onto the back porch, pulling the back door softly closed behind her.

The station wagon, of course, is unharmed, but still screaming, and Jack is long gone when Soles runs down the front steps and across the lawn to turn off the alarm.

Ng stays upstairs, fooled by the self-locking back door into thinking nobody went out that way.

Two figures, one of them in festive, tessellated, cow-themed sleepwear, vault the low picket fence into the adjacent backyard, and disappear.

nineteen

■

A still life: movie studio at midday. Pink-brown and paling. Dream within the dream. Scrawny oaks cluster in the walkways and courtyards of the producer's buildings, sleepy parking lots, empty streets, baked asphalt. A water tower that looms like just another abandoned idea.

Jack dodges a golf cart careening down the narrow alley between two massive sound stages on the Warner Bros., back lot.

"The cops will figure out you're here," Rachel is telling him, skipping to keep up. "They'll analyze the stuff in your apartment."

Jack says, "By the time my deal gets made? I'll be wrapped and gone." Jack hopes he's right. Cops in his apartment is a troubling development.

"I would never be an actor," Rachel responds, as if this logically follows her observation about the police. She wants to talk about anything but Murphy. "Because, in the first place, it's way too sketchy. And everyone's judging you. I'd want to be the director, so I could control what was happening and not be, like, some kind of thing that somebody else is always telling where to stand and what to say and how to say it." It took her a long time to stop crying about the cat. Her eyes are still red.

"I guess I'm lazy," Jack says.

Murphy wasn't, technically, Jack's cat. He showed up on the back porch during a thunderstorm, and Jack took him inside and dried him off and fed him some tuna from a can one of the girl-friends had left. For a few weeks after that, Murphy would come and go, disappearing for a week, then returning to howl at the back door. Jack looked for lost-pet posters on telephone poles and grocery store bulletin boards, asked the neighbors; no one seemed to know the cat, several seemed to think it had always been Jack's.

Eventually, Murphy just moved in, slept in a closet, gave Jack his attention only when he got hungry, or lonely, or bored.

He was, Jack thinks, a lot like me.

Murphy's dead. And Jack is blank and unreadable, walking across the studio lot.

"I grew up with television," Rachel continues, like some streaming podcast you can't turn off. This, Jack realizes, is her way of coping. Words. Jack is shaken by Murphy's death, but it is the consequence of what Jack does, manufacturing emotion where there is none, that causes him to simply shut down when confronted with the real thing. "My friends? It's like drugs. Tele-vision and Nintendo, AIM, Facebook, Xbox 360. I look at some of these little kids, they're like, put them in front of a flat screen and forget about it. Zombies."

Jack repeats, ironic: "You look at some of these kids?"

"What."

"You look at some of these kids."

"I don't get it."

A tanned, bearded second A.D. in fatigue pants and a backward Mets cap garnished with a cordless microphone headset cuts sharply around the corner on a fat-tire Schwinn and then jams on the brakes to leave a skid mark.

"Jack Baylor?" He hardly glances at the pajama pants. "Jack?" Jack nods, and he continues. "Evan. I'm the second-second." At Rachel, "Hi." And then, clocking her weepy eyes: "Allergies? I know. Sucks." Back to Jack: "You hungry?" And into his walkie-talkie: "Got him. Bring a B.B. to wardrobe, and alert God himself." To Jack, again: "Cheese and onions? Chili? Roach wagon's packing up, if we're gonna get you something we gotta get it now. Anything to drink?"

Jack looks at Rachel.

"B.B.?" she wonders, frowning.

"Breakfast burrito," Jack explains.

Rachel nods ever so slightly. "Full bag of groceries," she says, tossing it off, something she's heard Kenny say at Fatburger.

"I'm guessing my sister wants everything on hers," Jack translates for Evan as the second-second wheels his bike around. "Just some black coffee for me."

Riding so slowly now that his front wheel has to torque from side to side so he can keep his balance, Evan leads them through a maze of equipment, trucks, teamsters glued to folding chairs, honey wagons, and cables, to the wardrobe trailer.

Inside, a half hour later, Rachel sits hunched in a canvas director's chair, munching on her mother-of-all-burritos while Jack poses in front of a mirror, studying his bruised face and trying to memorize his part from three pink script pages.

"She's safe," Jack recites. "From you." A waifish omnisexual wardrobe assistant, something right out of Dickens, complete with a scarf looped around his/her neck, is at his feet, hemming a pair of black cotton slacks. The laconic wardrobe master is hanging Jack's pajama bottoms up on a fancy press.

"Why these are actual-in-fact jammies," he says with a syrupy Southern accent that even Rachel can tell is fake.

"Don't accept cheap substitutes," quips Jack. He's in his element here. Chill. Confident. Relaxed, for the first time in almost two days.

The wardrobe master crosses to him. "Shirt, please."

Jack takes his shirt off. He watches in the mirror as Rachel watches the wardrobe guy's eyes go over the road map of fresh scars on Jack's back, from Petty's beating.

"Oh, my."

"She had toenails like you can't believe," Jack quips. The wardrobe master looks at Rachel. "That's my sister," Jack adds. Rachel blushes, without quite knowing why.

"Don't say anything crass," the wardrobe guy warns his assistant. "Sister. Incest. Not funny. Just so you know."

"Never crossed my mind," the assistant says.

"Liar. You're Catholic."

"What does that have to do with it?"

"Doh. Incest. It's that, like—"

"No, no, you're thinking of pederasty. Different sin entirely."

The assistant, on his/her feet now, hands the wardrobe master a long-sleeved thermal undershirt and a denim tab-collar short-sleeved clergy shirt, which get briefly examined, considered, and then passed on to Jack, who frowns: "I'm a priest? Zorn is a lumberjack cleric?"

"Didn't used to be," sings the waif.

"Directorial vision, Jack," explains the wardrobe master. "Every day an adventure. His Majesty is way into Qabalah, and has these direct conversations with the Godhead about his movie. Don't even begin to ask."

The director himself, Chung Wiley, is black-bearded, balding, his long, stringy hair pulled back carefully in a vaguely chop-socky way and held with a rubber band. There's nothing Asian about him except his first name, which, Jack remembers from reading *The Defamer*, was coined in NYU film school. Incandescent red bloodshot double-vodka-with-a-twist eyes glowering out under the brim of a perfectly aged Red Sox cap pushed back on his head, Victor "Chung" Wiley is waiting on the set impatiently for Jack, despite the fact that Jack is fifteen minutes early for his call.

Wiley brushes a stray scrap of toilet paper off Jack's neck, as he murmurs importantly: "He's a man who has taken his eye off the divine curve ball, Jack. He's swinging and missing. His bat is cork at the center, you understand me? Suddenly it's only possible for him to say what God isn't."

Jack, for his part, listens to this somberly. There is a place Jack can go when he's acting, a quiet place of utter resignation, like a small child curled in the lap of a parent. It's warm and safe and the world falls away.

"He doesn't care what Frank wants," Wiley continues. "He lusts for the girl, and if he can't have her no one else can."

Jack nods, thinking suddenly of Mona. His chest tightens and even Wiley, lost in the genius of his own direction, notices.

"Jack? You with me? You ready?"

"I'm painting the inner picture," Jack says. He finds Rachel's face intent upon him from the dim netherworld of behind the camera. "Okay, yeah, let's do it."

The set on Stage 22 is a cabin, rustic and run-down. The surrounding scrim is a cheesy, painted, deeply leafy forest that Jack, like the camera lens, can't really differentiate from the real thing. A crudely carved crucifix on one wall, Christ's wearing buckskins and a coonskin cap. Empty bottles of alcohol. Ochre light from a color-gaffed 10K tungsten streaming through a window onto Jack, and the director, Wiley, who backs away, purring: "Economy. Everything and nothing. Nexus of divine energy. Keep it simple. This isn't brain surgery."

What am I doing here? Jack thinks, suddenly.

"Settle . . ."

"Camera's up!"

"Rolling."

"Speed." A slate bangs down, a grip barks out movie code for the preliminary try at the scene. The stillness, the quiet, always astonishes him.

". . . and action, Jack."

Action is Jack, sitting, channeling his inner ecclesiastic Bull of the Woods drunk, on a canvas cot.

At the studio's Hollywood Way gate, Deputies Soles and Ng are down the rabbit hole, and have no inkling of the Byzantine praxis into which they've unwittingly tumbled. They've followed their protocol and called ahead, informed studio security that they're coming, that Jack Baylor is a person of interest in a crime investigation, and requested that, should the suspect happen to show up on the set, they'd like him to be detained until their arrival. Soles, however, registers some disquieting confusion on the studio end about whether the suspect has, in fact, been hired; what Soles doesn't know, cannot be expected to know, is that film companies tend to operate like rogue forward combat units, usually a day or two ahead of central command, off the grid and in infrequent communication, owing to the time-honored ineluctable hostility between studio bean counters and on-set producers. The Chung Wiley film is two weeks behind schedule, ten million dollars over budget, and not even the first assistant director can be sure of what they'll be shooting next.

Soles and Ng have entered a parallel universe in which the only certainty is disappointment. Blissfully naive, they arrive in their station wagon and a beefy guard with a holstered gun that Soles doubts is real leans in at them, leading with aviator glasses that hide an idiot's eyes. Taking in their uniforms and badges.

"Twentynine Palms police?" The guard emits a low-watt grin. "Heh. You get those badges from props?"

"We need to go to Stage 22," Ng tells him, consulting scrawled notes. "We called ahead."

"Somebody there know you're coming?"

"We're sheriff's deputies from San Bernardino County, investigating a crime."

"Hoh. That doesn't sound made-up or anything."

"Excuse me?"

"I thought you said you were police."

"It's complicated. We're contract law enforcement, county to municipality—"

"Nice try. Turn around here and go to the Barham Gate, they've got the *Copville* SEG applications in a box. You wasted good money on the uniforms, though. Extras, they just look at your head shots and play eenie meenie moe."

"We're not here to be in *Copville*. Call your studio security office," Ng tells the guard, extending a business card to him through the window. "We talked to somebody named Mr. Bower."

"Bower," the fat guard grumbles. "Our power's out," he adds resentfully. "So I guess I'll have to use my personal phone."

On Stage 22, it's all gone bad.

It's bad because Chung Wiley has his arm around Jack's shoulder, and Jack is only a day player and directors do not like to touch day players and only do so when it's gone bad.

"It takes him a couple at-bats to find his groove," Wiley is telling Jack, as if they are old friends and the director feels obligated to apologize for the movie star sitting petulantly in the long-legged canvas chair among his own rogue state of makeup, wardrobe, and personal assistants. "The drugs have cut him off from his divine light, which flows from the unmanifested through the Keter into manifestation."

"Right. Well. I can just go with him," Jack proposes, never sure what this even means. "Sort of see where he's going, and, you know—"

"Go with it, no, no, no, Jack"—this is Wiley's nightmare, a day player with constructive ideas—"just keep doing what you're doing and he'll catch up by the time we get into coverage. You know: lightning flash. Each Sephirah, in turn, according to their enumerations."

"What?"

"Don't even think about it," Wiley says.

"Don't even think" is what Jack knows he means.

At the craft service table, Jack says no to the glazed donuts and pours himself another cup of black coffee. And then, suddenly, the movie star is beside him, as if to get coffee, but he has an assistant who does that, and only that, and exclusively from off-lot specialty coffee houses, so this can only be to have a conversation with Jack.

"I forgot your name."

Jack tells him.

"Right. Sorry. Jack. Listen. You know what we need, man," the movie star says amiably. "We need to loosen up a little. Fuck the hacky dialogue. You know that thing, we should do that thing, that thing where I'm like, 'Where is she?' and then you repeat me, 'Where is she?' And maybe I go, like, 'I love her,' and then you're, you know—"

"—I say what you say," Jack says. "I say, 'You love her?'"

"Right. Yes. Exactly. It's like, we're ad-libbing, kinda scatting-thing, or whatever."

"Improvising."

"Okay."

"If you kill me you'll never find her," Jack says, in character.

The movie star smiles. "Me? I'll never find her?"

"If I kill her."

"Kill her? You won't kill her."

"I won't kill her? Try me."

"I will."

"You will?"

"Fuckinlutely."

"You talking to me?"

"Are you talking to me? Cuz I'm most definitely talking to you."

Suddenly they're both doing bad De Niro, and the movie star is really into it, eyes darting around the sound stage to locate Wiley: "Chungage? Yo yo yo, Chung, man, get your bony ass over here."

Chungage? Jack wonders if Mr. Wiley lets regular people mangle his carefully honed Pan-Asiatic handle.

But Chung Wiley comes dutifully to the donut table, trying to retain his imperial bearing, but cowed by the multimillion-dollar size of the movie star's ego. He listens politely to a suggestion he's heard before, how to irreversibly dilute his taut cabin scene and turn it into an editorial nightmare in one easy lesson. "All the paths are numbered," he keeps saying. "All the paths are numbered."

And Jack is in a crush of fatigue. The shadows of the desert are catching up with him. Something has snapped, and he can't find that peaceful, passive place; his eye aches, his ability to find depth has ditched him again. When he looks around now he sees only the cardboard cutouts of a sound stage, crew, and movie set. A sixth-grade shoebox diorama. He interrupts, impatient, tentative, low-key. "Could we—could I suggest something? I had this thought. Some dialogue, it's minor—something I overheard the other day—" Not only has Jack interrupted the principal actor and director's argument, he's talking principally to Chung Wiley, leaving the movie star with nothing to do with his hands except find the box of sugar cubes by the coffee thermos and eat squares, one by one.

"What if, after he slams me against the wall, I just say something like, 'You feel guilty about it. You confuse this with love.' You know? Or, even, 'Love is selfless, my friend. It's not an act of contrition. It wants nothing. Nothing.'"

There is a wired pause, and Wiley stares at Jack strangely, differently than he has before.

"'The Spirit itself beareth witness with our spirit that we are the children of God,'" Jack adds, remembering the pastor's quotation, but still not clear on the meaning of it.

"Jesus, check the gate," Wiley says, meaning that he likes it. He looks at his movie star.

"He can't say that."

"Why not?" Wiley says, forgetting the game for a moment. "It's smart. It takes the scene to another level."

Just plain pissed now, the movie star won't look at Jack. He's walking away, past the camera and assembled crew and Rachel in her chair.

"He can't say that." He points back at Wiley, whirling, walking backward, "If that gets said, I get to say it."

"It doesn't make sense for you to say it, yo."

"I get the last line in the scene, Chung! Not some fucking one-day wonder!"

Now Wiley looks regretfully at Jack. They both overplayed their hands, they both understand why the other did it, and in this shared crime they find a moment of solace.

Only a moment.

Then it becomes Jack's mistake, and Jack's alone. Wiley dons the threadbare imperial directorial, gestures pantomime to the Qabalah God overhead, *Ain Suph Aur*, letting the crew know, in a strong but likeable way, that he's one of them, and, yes, Asshole got the film financed and gave them their jobs, but if we could kill him and stuff him or replace him with CGI and get away with it we would.

"That's a wrap," he calls out, and the crew falls into its quiet, efficient routine, shutting the set down for the day. Lights off, cables coiled, scrims stowed, wardrobe racks rolling into the sound stage shadows.

"You a writer?" Chung asks Jack.

"No."

"You've got good ideas," he says. "Maybe we should talk about you writing something for me."

"Meaning I'm fired," Jack interprets.

Chung chews a nail. "Yeah."

At the gate, Soles and Ng are still waiting. For a while, another guard, slender, dimple-chinned like an old fashioned B-movie leading man, was waving traffic around them, but now they've pulled to the side, into special parking apparently reserved for visitors in guard-gate limbo, since there are three spaces in anticipation of even more institutional dysfunction. Their personal studio guard is on the phone in the little wood-and-glass kiosk where, in a Grimm's fairy tale, he would live. He's nodding.

"That's a good sign," Soles observes.

The guard is nodding and talking.

"You think so?"

"I do. I'm an optimist."

"How much you think these guys make?" Ng wonders.

"Enough to live on," says Soles. "In the Valley."

"As much as us?"

"Doubtful. It's not a skilled job, Vince. It's just this side of reception."

The guard finally hangs up, unimpressed. Fiddles around, irritably, in the kiosk as something spits out of a vintage dot-matrix printer, then spends another few minutes carefully removing the track-feed punch holes from either side of it. Finally he steps outside, slaps a pass on their windshield, and says, "Follow the green line, park in an unmarked space. You'll be looking for Stage 22, all the way down and left." He emphasizes the *two* in *twenty-two*, just to let them know that he's still the man.

"Thanks," Ng says. "Is that gun real?"

But Soles has driven away before Ng can get his answer.

Everyone is leaving.

Nobody says anything to Jack. He's the invisible man. He sips his cold coffee and Rachel waits impatiently for him to make a decision. Ordinarily, Jack would be in no hurry to go. Ordinarily, Jack is more comfortable on a movie set than anywhere else, cloistered, secure, everything provided: food, clothing, what to say, where to stand, when to sit. He doesn't have to think. Only misfortune awaits him outside the Warner Bros.' lot fences and walls. He looks at Rachel and wonders if he could get somebody on the crew to take her home. This depresses him. He can't take care of her, he couldn't take care of Murphy, he wouldn't take care of Mona, he won't even take care of himself.

Evan, the second-second, materializes out of the darkness with a chubby, letter-sized envelope. "Your agent sent this by messenger. Feels like a payday, compadre."

"Thanks. You got a cigarette?"

Evan does, of course, and Jack takes it, along with the book of matches Evan kindly offers, saying, "Your idea ripped, man. I am so sorry." Jack wouldn't be surprised if a second-second were carrying a Virginia ham and a smoker oven somewhere on his person.

"Don't worry about it. Shit happens." Jack's never said *shit happens* before. He falls into a deeper funk and they stand in an awkward silence, Evan on unsure footing now, since Jack has, basically, become toxic and ceased to exist.

"You waiting here for those cops?"

Jack stares at him.

"I bet they got held up at the gate. You know, the usual drive-on bullshit. You in real trouble, brother, or is it, like, parking tickets or some stupid shit?"

Cops at the gate.

Fortunately, Evan's walkie-talkie squawks, and with an apologetic nod he hurries away. Jack taps the cigarette on the back of his hand and wills himself into motion and starts across the sound stage, through the cabin set, toward the big stage doors, as if to have his smoke outside.

"Jack?" Rachel follows him. Outside, the Valley heat hits

them, and under the huge stenciled 22 on the soundstage wall, Jack turns toward the edge of the lot.

"Jack?" Rachel struggles to keep pace with him. Jack doesn't acknowledge her, doesn't look back. They find cover behind some portable generators parked against a twelve-foot-high chain-link fence topped by razor wire, which runs half a mile in either direction along the concrete rim of the trapezoidal L.A. River.

"Jack—"

"Cops. Don't follow me. I'm sorry." He fumbles for some money from the envelope in his pants, drops it, picks it up again, presses a hundred dollars into her hands and stows the rest. He starts to climb the fence. He's near to panic.

"I don't want your money. You can't just leave me here," Rachel says. "Don't be a dick. What am I supposed to do? What am I supposed to tell them?"

Early in his career, Jack went to the Academy Awards, as a seat filler. During the commercials, when a famous person got up to go to the bathroom or get a drink or just from utter boredom, Jack would be hustled down the aisle to fill the seat so that, when the cameras came back up on the audience, the house would be packed.

He sat next to a girl, barely seventeen, who'd been abducted in Nashville at age eight by some righteous wingnut and raped and locked up and then later forced into prostitution to support his ministry as he traveled blue highways baptizing unsuspecting small-town believers. Fox Searchlight made a movie about her life; the actress who portrayed her was nominated for an Academy Award, and sat on the other side of her, holding her hand. The girl wore a beautiful dress and expensive jewelry, and her eyes shone and she couldn't stop smiling. The producers were sending her to college, she wanted to be an actress, she had a small role in her film, she'd been reunited with her mom and sister. Happy endings, Jack thought, until he heard, later, that at the Governor's Ball after the awards ceremony, she'd been approached by a number of men—agents, managers, development executives—who gave her their business cards and got her number and their only question was, basically, "How much?"

"Jack?" Rachel is looking up at him.

"I am a dick," he announces. "I'm from the planet of dicks. We see in two dimensions and believe in nothing. That's how I can leave you here with a fistful of cash. That's why you can't go with me," Jack says, from near the top of the fence. He looks at the razor wire skeptically, though, and wonders where the hell he thinks he's going. On the other side of the fence, if he ever gets there, the cement trough pitches down at sixty degrees to a trickle of gutter runoff and, here and there, a weed or a hubcap.

Rachel clambers up the fence beside Jack, quicker than he is. "I'm not going with you," Rachel says. There are tears in her eyes again, but she's not crying. "I'm taking you with me." She pulls off her sundress, revealing a leotard top and spandex shorts. Throws the sundress up over the wire, covering it, then scrambles across it and down the other side. "There's some sharp spots," she warns Jack.

Chastened, and much more slowly, he negotiates the wire, getting his pants tangled twice before he finds toeholds on the other side. Jack drops and slides down into the flood channel.

Rachel is still up above, at the fence, jumping up and down, struggling to disentangle her dress.

Jack looks toward the insult of sun pinned just above the Santa Monica Mountains like a life you look back at. He wants to walk, run, get away.

But he waits for Rachel.

* * *

Idling in their wagon down the crowded rows of long, looming stages, Soles and Ng are already lost.

"Down . . . and left?" Soles wonders.

"Here's Stage 8," Ng says.

A guy on a bicycle comes rolling past them, with a film canister shoved under one arm.

"Excuse me—hey—" Soles leans out and shouts after him.

The bicyclist circles, comes back to them, but never stops.

Soles asks, "Where's Stage 22?"

The bicyclist grabs onto a door handle and lets the car pull him. Gesturing with his free hand and nearly falling off: "I think it's that way. Yeah. Two streets." He surges away, pedaling.

"Thank you," Ng says.

The two deputies turn left and head down a narrow alley between some short stages, only to find themselves cut off by an enormous double-wide trailer with a pop-out wedged into the passageway. A woman in a tiny bikini lies on a lounge chair reading *Vanity Fair*.

Ng puts the car in reverse, doubles back, and they are quickly lost again. By the time they get to the set, there will be a few grips and carpenters playing liar's poker on the empty craft service table, and none of them will be able to say whether the actor Jack Baylor was even on the set today.

twenty

■

Something fundamental has changed. Jack pulls out from Valley Bob's Used Cars into crosscurrents of traffic, seven hundred dollars poorer but in possession of a rumbling, brown, two-and-a-half-ton 1972 Pontiac Bonneville, with Turbo Hydramatic transmission, 455 cubic inch V8, and a peeling Cordova roof. Rachel is slumped down beside him in the passenger's seat, the way she does on the ride to school.

"This guy I told you about, Buck, he's had this juvie shelter in Santa Barbara for about five years," Jack says after a couple minutes of dead air. "We used to tear it up when we were in high school, so I guess he understands what would make somebody want to run away from home."

Rachel says nothing. She tries to turn on the radio, but it doesn't work.

"You'll like him," Jack continues.

"Your surf buddy?"

"No, that was Tory. I haven't surfed for a long time," Jack adds.

Rachel's voice breaks, just barely. "I thought we made a good team."

Jack looks at her. He's struck all at once by how young she is, just a kid, absolutely, for all her wit and attitude, she's still a kid. And it hits him: "We make a great team because you're pretty grown-up for your age and I'm about twenty years slow. But, long run, be realistic, that dog won't hunt."

Rachel just stares out the side window.

"Where will you go?"

"There's two choices here, Rachel. Either I drop you off with Buck at his halfway house in Santa Barbara, or I take you home to your parents. Maybe I can talk to them for you. If your old man tries anything, I can take a poke at him, you know, or sucker punch him. He's gotta be a pushover compared to the cops and that old marine."

"I hate you."

"You want me to talk to your mom, about—"

"You said you'd take care of me."

"I'm sorry."

"You won't hit anybody."

"I might." Sigh. "But probably not, no."

"I hate you."

"Okay."

"I do."

"Okay."

Jack waits. Rachel knows he's waiting. "Take me home," she says, finally, and gives him low, terse directions to a shady street in Brentwood, deep in the bowels of upper-middle-class bliss. Fresh McMansions nestled in forests of lush non-indigenous

flora, ferns, palms, live oak, and magnolia trees. Jack's mud-
brown Bonneville belongs here only when a non-English-speak-
ing housekeeper drives herself to work. The house at which
Rachel tells him to stop is a sleek, low-slung, ranch-style split-
level on steroids, with a shake roof and cherrywood shutters and
a broad, green, flawless front lawn with riotous oleander hedges
and a solar sundial and a Range Rover in the driveway.

"This. This is where you live?"

"I know."

"Fuck."

"I know." Rachel struggles with her seat belt. It's stuck. Jack
helps her get it free. "What about it?"

"I just thought—when you told me about, you know, your
dad and everything—"

"Okay, yes, I was sort of lying." Rachel pushes open her door,
but doesn't get out. "I didn't think you'd actually believe me."
Rachel looks back at Jack, tears in her eyes.

"Your old man doesn't—?"

"No. He's okay. I mean. You know." She sucks her lip. "I had
this fight, at school, with my boyfriend? Sully? Who's like pretty
annoying and everything, and thinks the whole world hates him,
but, you know—and my Dad goes, basically, 'What's the big
deal, sweetiepie, you're only fourteen years old and it's not like
you're going to marry him or anything.'" Rachel looks away and
kicks at the door and it swings out heavily, and then comes back
to her foot. The neighborhood is quiet. Safe. "So I ran away."

"Are your parents really my age?"

"What difference does it make?"

Jack just stares at her, lost.

"But, I mean, it was important," Rachel insists defensively,
"to me. Some things are really important, that's all. Just because

I'm fourteen doesn't make it not important. I mean, what if I don't even make it to fifteen? What's important now is going to be the most important thing that will ever happen to me."

"You lied about everything."

"No. Not everything."

"Oh, it's okay then."

"I didn't think you'd take me with you if I told you the truth."

"You're right. I wouldn't have."

"See?" Rachel looks at her house. "Think they're gonna ground me?"

"Rachel," Jack says, starting down a very adult path of illuminative instruction, but losing his way immediately, and settling for, "you can't run away from stuff."

"Doh, Jack."

Jack decides not to say anything else on the subject. Rachel is staring at her house.

"They're gonna ground me."

"Was it worth it?"

The front door of the house opens, and a woman emerges. She has Rachel's coloring and stubborn mouth.

"You didn't do it."

"No, I didn't."

"You gotta prove you didn't."

"Unfortunately, I don't have any idea how I'd do that."

The woman calls out, "Rachel?"

Rachel looks back at Jack. "I gotta go. Write me or something, okay? Just so I know, you know, that you're good and everything."

"Yeah."

Rachel gets out, slams the car door shut, then runs across the lawn to her mother, who embraces her, tearfully, far more relieved than angry. Jack starts his car. A man comes out onto the porch. Rachel's father. He's tall, and doesn't look all that much older than Jack. He embraces his daughter openly, warmly, like someone who genuinely cares more about her than where she's been, and it's all too much for Jack, who puts the car in gear and drives away.

In the rearview mirror he can see Rachel and her parents go inside the house. And only after they're gone, and Jack turns the corner, does he become acutely aware of the strange loopy smile that's been on his face since he started the car.

twenty-one

■

On the black dream of coastal highway north of Ventura, the Bonneville floats on soft springs, cruising beside an ocean blurred by fog into which the day has expired.

At the shrouded Montecito turnoff, Jack stands in a gas station phone booth, waiting for his call to connect. Waiting. Waiting.

"Come on, Jilly. Answer the phone."

She doesn't.

A highway sign materializes out of the brume: LA CUMBRE ROAD. 2 MILES. It slides past, into darkness, and is gone. In the flush green glow from the dashboard, Jack's face floods with indecision.

* * *

The fog holds light, gives it dimly to the Hope Ranch overpass as Jack's Bonneville cruises past. Brake lights punch the dark. He pulls over and stops on the shoulder, two hundred yards past the La Cumbre on-ramp, and a moment passes. Then another. Jack's mind whirls. The familiar grip of Tory Geller clutches at Jack's resolve.

A rat-colored Cayman comes down the on-ramp, engine winding out, and disappears down the highway.

White back-up lights flare. Jack starts to reverse his big car, on the shoulder. He backs all the way to the on-ramp, all the way up the on-ramp, backwards, and then onto the street. He stops then, and starts across the overpass, in no real hurry now, headed for Hope Ranch.

Classic California emerging from a pall.

Dreams dislodged, out of time, suspended.

Orange trees. Walnut. Plum. The fruit orchard.

Broken-down asphalt tennis court, net sagging, cracks corrupted by sow thistle and punagrass. Spanish walls. Terracotta tile.

Five-car garage, with a chauffeur's apartment overhead. Looming farther back above the parking circle, guarded by overgrown trees, just the suggestion of a Mission-style mansion. The lights are all out, the windows cold and black.

Jack's Bonneville pulls up behind a white BMW convertible. He kills the headlights, steps out into the cool night air.

It's very quiet. Far off in the darkness a gentle surf crawls over coarse sand. The thick fog softens everything around Jack. He walks up a long stone walkway to the front door of the big house, rings the doorbell.

Waits.

Knocks loudly.

Waits.

Then he steps back and looks up at the windows of the second floor: still lifeless, still dark.

But there is a light piercing through the fog, from behind him. Jack turns and looks at the garage. Five double-door garages, mocked up like stables, someone's idea of high style. One of the windows of the apartment above the double doors glows yellow. Jack wanders down the driveway, drawn to it.

Between two of the individual car bays there is a dark opening, a passageway with steps leading up to the apartment. Only when his eyes adjust does Jack notice that the door at the top of the stairs is propped open. A very dim light spills out and down. Jack slowly climbs the stairs.

The outer room of the big apartment is unlit, cluttered with saggy old furniture. This is where antiques go to die, Jack says to himself, in Tory's voice, because it's something Tory always says.

There's light in the bedroom, and movement, a shadow on the far wall. Jack carefully makes his way through the maze of furniture.

The bedroom is relatively empty, a steel bed frame, bare mattress, matching deco maple bureau, vanity, and nightstand. The sour smell of dust and decay, mold in the walls, damp carpet, desiccated lace curtains. Hannah Geller has positioned herself in front of the bay window, looking out at the misty orchard.

"I watched you drive up. I wondered who it could be, in that car."

Jack stays in the doorway, wary, waits for Hannah to turn around. She doesn't. She's wearing a black cocktail dress, high heels, fat pearls.

"Remember the night we did it up here, Jack? Tory was drunk. He was out there, in the orchard. Calling for us. I stood right here. Kind of bent over. You were behind me. Insert tab A in slot B. Repeat as necessary. God. My knees shook. I got a splinter in my hand. We did it while Tory, remember, while he wandered through those spent old plum trees, calling our names."

"I felt sorry for you."

"The pity fuck. There's a compliment every girl likes to hear."

"That's not what I meant."

"You're not good at this, are you?" She puts both hands on the windowsill and arches her back and neck, rolling her shoulders languidly. "Tory says you're a dancer."

"I don't know what that means, but he's wrong, I don't—"

"Always in motion, always dipping, turning, backing away."

"Oh."

"Is that right?"

"Tory's known me for a long time."

"Not nearly well enough, though, huh?"

"Things change."

"Do they? I didn't think you would. I don't think Tory has."

"I can only see with one eye."

"And?"

"Two dimensions."

"I have no fucking idea what you're talking about."

"Where's Tory now?" Jack asks.

"Out." She turns. "You never danced with me." There's a bottle of vodka, and a cut-crystal rocks glass, half full, no ice, on the wide sill of the latticed window. Now Jack sees the rudely obvious stitches on Hannah's wrists. She actually turns her hands so that he can't miss them, and so that she can enjoy his shock and dismay.

"They told me, at the hospital that, next time"—she mimes slicing her wrist with an imaginary razor blade—"this way. Not across the wrist. Lengthwise." She laughs mirthlessly. "I didn't realize there was a technique involved. You know, there's a whole subculture of bipolar suicidal bloggers online. I've made a bunch of new friends. My screen name is Hannahbanana."

"How much lousier do you want me to feel?"

"How bad can I make it? No—even worse than that. Worse than me, anyway."

"Tory knows?" It crosses Jack's mind that Tory could have done this, or that they both could have worked it up, as a conversation piece, as another piece of outrageousness in case anybody had forgotten that Hannah and Tory were volatile.

"Tory found me," Hannah says carelessly. "Blood everywhere," she adds.

"Did you tell him about us?"

"Tell him what?" Hannah's trying to make Jack squirm with coy answers to questions Jack doesn't really need to ask. She shakes a Sherman out of a box on the side table and puts it between her lips. Jack sees that she's drunker than he first thought. Her gestures have a bluntness that gives her away. "You're not driving the car I bought for you. You're not wearing the boots I gave you for Christmas."

"I'm not that guy anymore."

"Oh? Who are you now? You probably don't even have our fucking lighter on you."

"Hannah."

"You should stay with me until Tory gets back. He'll want to see you."

Jack mumbles something about not knowing what he'd say to him, but Hannah doesn't care what he has to say.

"How 'bout this," she says, and lowers her voice to a fair imitation of Jack as performed by a drunken woman, "sorry I screwed your wife, Tory. Oh yeah, and sorry I screwed you." Hannah gulps vodka, flashes a wired smile. "Something sincere.

You'll think of it, Jack. You're a pro." She reaches back and unzips her dress and lets it puddle on the floor at her feet.

Jack suddenly decides he's got to get out of the house. "You don't love me, Hannah. You just got bored with your husband."

Hannah says nothing for a long time. She sits down on the bed and puts her hands back and stretches, her perfect breasts lifting and shifting, her hair falling away. "It's kind of funny. But. Lying in the bathtub? My wrists in the warm water, to, you know. Well. I've got to admit it, Jack, I did wonder what you'd say. When you found out." Hannah does her Jack bit again, flat and emotionless. "Something like: 'Hey. She's dead.' No. I don't know. Something underwhelming, though, don't you think?"

"Oh, get off my back!" Jack explodes at her. "We both did this! I didn't come on to you every time Tory was drunk, or fucked up! We made mistakes! Both of us!"

Hannah lies back heavily on the sagging mattress, hands toying with her hair, frowning. "Wait. You don't think . . . ? Jack, I didn't cut my wrists over you. I want him back. I did it for Tory." She draws her knees up and folds them to one side, sleazy demure.

Flashbulbs pop in Jack's brain and his neck stiffens.

Hannah laughs. "My God. Oh, you poor, self-centered little bastard."

"That's me," Jack says.

Hannah smiles grimly, breathtakingly beautiful, and magnificently wrong. "You know what I think? I think he was more upset that you'd thrown me over—pissed on his woman, that sort of thing—than he was at finding out we were lovers."

"Where did he go?" Jack asks, very scared now. Random pieces fall together in his mind. The hollow horror of an answer he wasn't even looking for.

"You know how he gets," she continues, oblivious, "he came home, there I was in the tub. My grand gesture. He freaked completely."

"Where did Tory go, Hannah?"

"Oh, to the desert, Jack." Hannah lets both wrists flutter in an operatic gesture, over her head, all Bette Davis. "He said he was going to kill you."

twenty-two

■

His nervous hands drum the steering wheel.

Remembering the blood everywhere.

And Mona.

Mona dying, Mona dead, and Jack's brown Bonneville races back through the darkness of the high desert to where he started. A passing eighteen-wheeler sucks a wall of wind behind it that rocks the car off onto the shoulder, where the tires rattle over reflectors and the corrugated safety stripe shakes Jack angrily out of his grim reflections. He steers his car back into the groove of his lane, blistered pavement, and darkness everywhere.

Somewhere in the endless smear of dark desert, Jack stops at a self-serve pump to fill his car with gas. He's lost track of time. He has only destination. He's adrift in his thoughts, moving by instinct, and habit.

The Mojave air is thick, strangely humid. Jack can taste the whole day's unleaded gas disgorged in it. A pale pickup truck with military plates fills, unattended, at the side-lot island, out of Jack's line of sight. Someone forgot to turn off the headlights, and they strobe a park service SUV as it pulls into the station and drives right on past the pumps.

Jack deliberately turns his back to them, remembering a scene where he had to do this once, a basic cable cop show. He was on the run from two bounty hunters, who were the stars. After a number of routine stunts, they caught him.

The SUV parks in front of the snack shop. Two men in mismatched uniforms get out: Park Ranger Petty, and Sheriff's Deputy Soles.

"Serial killer, mark my words," Petty is saying, and then they go inside, jiggling the happy bell on the front door.

Lightning splits the sky. There is a leaden rumble of thunder moments later. Jack's throat is tight, his pulse quick. He tries to recall the formula for figuring out how far away a storm is by timing the space between the light and the noise. When he was little he would lie in bed and count one-alligator, two-alligator, three-alligator.

He waits for another flash of lightning, more than ready to count.

Inside the snack shop, Petty beelines for the microwave food station. Soles grabs some Halls throat lozenges and queues at the check-out counter, behind a stocky man, ex-military, Soles decides, probably a non-com marine, from the haircut, wearing a STAY BLYTHE! T-shirt and buying a fairly desperate assortment of Tums, Pepto-Bismol, Mylanta, Maalox, and other stomach treatments.

"Y'all wasted your time going to Lost Angeles," Petty says.

Some fool left their lights on, Soles thinks, looking out at the pumps and the pale truck.

"Next time we see him," Petty continues, gloating, from the snack bar, "he'll be on one of those 'America's Most Gruesome Sex Crimes' shows or something. They'll probably want to interview one of us about it, too."

Thunder murmurs outside. Petty pops a patty and bun into the microwave oven, fires it up. Soles debates whether he should tell Petty about the preliminary results of the blood from the crime scene, and how it doesn't belong to the alleged victim, Mona Malloy, but fusses some phlegm in his throat instead. The big man in front of him, just finishing his pharmaceutical transaction at the cash register, is wearing a very familiar pair of Larry Mahan boots. It's Symes. He turns to go, face chalky, still sick.

"Probably me," Petty is saying, continuing his earlier line of thought, "since I had the closest encounter with said suspect." The ray oven buzzes, hamburger inside steaming hot. "No, he's long gone, Soles. *Adios, muchacho. Hasta la vista.*"

Before he gets to the door, something Symes sees outside stops him short. It's his headlights, poor guy's just realized he left them on, Soles guesses, and then steps to the register.

"What makes 'em hard to catch is the sheer audacity of the crime," Petty winds on and on as he plunders the garnish tray. "They're sociopaths. See, they don't think they've even done anything wrong."

The cashier rings up Soles' purchase, and he gives her his full attention because suddenly the register is doing the talking. "Eighty-nine. Eighty-nine. Eighty-nine. Sales tax. Two dollars and ninety-three cents."

"Good Lord," Soles remarks.

"Ain't it the shit?" the cashier grumbles. "We're inching closer to the world's end every damn day."

Soles gives the cashier three dollars, takes his seven cents, then, frowning slightly as if he's just remembered what he came for, looks back out the window at the pumps.

The Bonneville is gone. The big man, Symes, is running to his truck. A bottle of Maalox splatters chalk-white on the asphalt. He doesn't even break stride.

twenty-three

■

The Bonneville moves slowly down a rutted gravel road. A cluster of silver mailboxes flickers past. Jack kills the headlights, and the car coasts over a flat stretch, then turns onto a narrower, hard-packed dirt driveway that curls up through the smoke tree, juniper, and Goodding willow on the gentle hillside.

Lightning splinters across the sky.

Jack urges his car about another hundred feet, switches the engine off, and rolls into the heavy brush that covers the hillside, until the car bottoms out, well concealed. Thunder breaks, close by now. Jack struggles to get out on his side of the car, but the door is wedged against a massive cholla tree and won't even budge. Frustrated, he slides to the passenger side, only to discover that door also blocked, so he squeezes out the window and into the business end of a double-barrel shotgun.

Symes presses the weapon against Jack's forehead so hard it stamps two perfect red circles in the skin.

Jack says, "Oh Jesus." He believes he's going to die.

Symes grabs Jack by the shirt, and half drags him out of the brush, to the middle of the dirt driveway.

"I didn't kill her. I swear to you that I didn't."

More lightning and thunder, not even seconds apart.

And Symes squats suddenly, grimacing. Doubled up by a twisting, wracking pain in his gut. "Godalmighty!" The gun drops, and Symes is sick, dry heaving, jackknifed by violent spasms. He wails like a baby.

Rain begins to fall. Big, hot drops that slap the dry ground and sting Jack's exposed face and arms. The shotgun has been abandoned by Symes, who lies in the grass, curled up like a fetus, eyes open. Helplessly, he watches Jack get the gun. The excruciating pain has passed, but he's too weak to do anything but breathe.

Jack holds the shotgun like somebody who's never actually held a real one but thinks they know how it's done. "Are those my boots?"

"No." Symes shakes his head, very tired. "I bought 'em from a guy in Calexico after you run off. He said he got 'em from a preacher."

Jack walks away.

At the bottom of the driveway he stops and looks up at the rhombus of shadow that is a structure higher up on the hill. Waiting. The rain is steady now, the wind has disappeared. Jack comes back to Symes, and puts the shotgun down.

"Why didn't you just shoot me?"

"That's not how I roll," Symes says, and there's no irony in it.

"The man who killed Mona is in that house up there," Jack says to Symes. "I'm going to go get him. If I can, I'll take him to the cops."

Symes just stares at him, blinking away the raindrops.

Jack wipes his own face with a wet sleeve, and detours into

the creosote and blackbrush to his car, opens the trunk and looks inside. He rummages under the spare tire and comes up with a rusty lug wrench.

"What good's that gonna do?" Symes is behind him, with the shotgun pointed down at the ground.

"I don't know," Jack says. "But if I take that gun up there it's more than likely I'll get killed with it than I'll do anybody else any harm."

Symes shivers violently. His voice is raw with emotion. "Did you sleep with her?"

"I did," Jack says.

It's hard to tell whether Symes is crying or it's just rain running down from the sides of his eyes. Jack doesn't want to think the big marine is crying.

"Did you love her?"

"Look, I don't—"

"It's just a question, son," Symes says.

"Yeah."

"Yes, what?"

"Yes . . . sir?"

Symes rolls his eyes. "What is wrong with you?"

"Yeah," Jack says. "I mean. I think I did. I thought I did."

"It isn't that complicated, Jack," Symes notes wearily, and Jack and Symes start walking up the hill together.

As the vegetation thins, they are confronted, fifty yards ahead, by a crooked house, stark and modern.

A crooked house. Symes blinks rain away, and says he thinks he's hallucinating. The windows are dark, no two of them alike, no two square with each other or even with their own opposite sides. Poured concrete walls rise at strange angles to a flat roof with no gutters. It's a house built either by a genius, or a three-year-old practicing how to make squares.

Jack is thinking about what's inside. He's been here before. In another life.

A faint light glows suddenly, deep within one of the unlikely windows. Moves. Disappears.

The two men move cautiously forward, across the open ground in front of the house. A sleek white Thunderbird is parked like an afterthought in front of the house. Jack crouches behind the car. Vanity plates: TORY G. There are dark, slippery handprints and smears on the trunk and bumper. Not mud. Starting to wash away in the rain. Jack looks up at Symes. "Let me go in the front door and try to talk to him. You go around and in the back. You're my insurance."

"Talk to him?"

"I know him. He's a friend of mine."

"Was."

"Was."

"And he's gonna want to talk to you?"

"Yeah." Jack can see Symes is skeptical. "What do you care if he kills me?"

Symes disappears around the back of the house. Jack goes up the front steps and tries the door. It's locked, but Jack knows where the spare key is hidden. He digs in the right side of one of the cactus planters and finds a bottle with a key in it. The dead-bolt unlocks and Jack opens the front door a crack, listening for movement inside, then cautiously eases through, and closes the door behind him with a click.

There is the hush of rain from outside, the rumble of rain-fall on the roof, the sound of water rutting down the windows. Lightning flashes through the skylights momentarily, revealing spooky orthogonal geometries wrapped in plaster, and soaring ceilings. Thunder shakes the house to its foundation.

In the silence that follows, Jack can hear the sound of water dripping off him and onto the carpet, and light, fleet, futtering footsteps across carpet and then tile. Jack whirls. Sees nothing. Crouches, scared again.

"Tory?"

Someone is behind Jack.

He pivots again, swinging the lug wrench blindly, missing his target completely. The wrench punctures the wall, and stays there, stuck fast. Something thin and blunt stabs Jack in the stomach, punching the wind out of him. He takes a step backward, trips, and the blunt object smacks him again.

"Ow!"

He falls to one knee, groping for anything to catch himself. A vase shatters on the tile floor. Someone giggles nervously. A light comes on, and Jack finds himself squinting up at two children he knows: Carrie and Zach. The boy feints with a broom handle. The little girl has her hand stretched to the light switch; she thinks it's a game.

"Carrie, turn out the light!" Mona steps from a hallway, lower lip blue and swollen, one leg and forearm crudely bandaged, a black Bersa Thunder 380 held with both hands, and aimed right at Jack's face. She doesn't recognize him. "Don't move, don't talk!" she shouts. The light goes out, plunging everything into a darkness from which, after a moment, comes a different version of the same voice. Softer. As if afraid to believe it: "Jack?"

Jack finds himself thinking, absurdly, that it's a perfect line reading of a single word. He'd like to hear it again. "Yeah. It's Jack."

There is a click that Jack guesses might be the safety on the gun. A shadow resolving itself into Mona lets the shape of the gun drop wearily to her side. She doesn't move. Jack gets to his feet. The broom handle pokes at him again, but this time he bumps it away.

"Don't do that," he warns the boy, and at the same moment more lightning backlights a figure poised at the rear door. Symes. Panicked, Jack scoops the boy up in one arm, lunges at the little girl and takes them both to the floor, screaming, "GET DOWN!" at Mona, whereupon Symes opens fire, blowing out the glass, ripping away most of the blinds. He hurtles through the opening, following his first salvo. Mona disappears, screaming. Jack covers both children. Symes rolls, all technique now, comes up and fires again, blowing a head-sized chunk out of the corner of the drywall above Jack, then starts to reload in the ensuing silence, before Jack finds his voice, "Symes! Don't shoot! Don't shoot!"

Symes turns it off as swiftly as he turned it on. "Roger that."

The little girl is crying.

"It's all right," Jack says to her. "It's all right. Mommy's right over there—" But Carrie is inconsolable, twists away from Jack and finds her mother in the darkness as if by instinct. Zach scoots under a table, with his broom, too stunned to make a sound.

Thunder rolls across the room.

"Talk to me, asshole. I can't see for shit."

"We're clear. There's nobody in here but friendlies."

Jack feels Mona's eyes on him. He hears her disengage herself from Carrie. Jack is up from the floor, on his knees, waiting, half expecting her to crawl over and kiss him or something, make some form of loving gesture, appropriate for his unexpected return, but when she finds him she kicks him hard in the groin and smacks him across the side of the head as he goes down sideways.

"You son of a bitch! You did this! You brought all this with you!"

Symes knows the voice. "Mona?"

She kicks Jack again, but her heart's not really in this one. Spiderweb lightning glints across skylights and her cheeks glisten with tears. Jack can't speak, can't breathe. The searing pain in his pelvis is nothing compared to the shame he feels. The utter defeat.

"What have you done to me?" Mona asks him. "What have you done to me? What have you done to me?"

Jack waits for a blow that doesn't come.

There is distant thunder and another silence, an easing of the rainfall on the metal roof, during which Symes breaks open his shotgun, and sidles closer, until he can make out Mona in the darkness, and she can see the astonishment on his face.

Mona talks softly, to her children: "Zach, take Carrie back into the bedroom please." The boy does so. He holds his sister's hand. When they're safely away, Mona looks down at Jack again, and murmurs, "Get up and get out." She adds, to Symes, more gently, "You can stay."

"Everyone thinks you're dead," Symes says.

"I could have been."

"Everyone thinks I killed you," Jack says, one hand down the front of his water-soaked pants, cradling his balls firmly, to make sure they haven't been detached from his person. "You and your kids. They think I cut you up and buried you somewhere out in the desert, and they want to fry me for it."

Mona leans back against the wall. Tired. A wind spits rain through the broken back door, and the storm gathers momentum again. "Not your style, Jack?"

Jack pushes himself upright, painfully. "You kick like a girl."

"I guess I would."

"Oh Lordy—where's the can?" Symes is doubled over again.

"Second door," Mona tells him.

Symes rushes across the room and disappears through a doorway.

Jack just stares at Mona. "I guess Tory's not at home?"

Mona stares back, sadly. Softly, she says, "No."

An interior light comes on as the trunk lid opens to reveal the stiff, folded-up, very dead carcass of Tory Geller. His skin is bloated and yellow-green. His neck has been punctured inelegantly on the jugular side by a nine-millimeter jacketed hollow-point bullet that appears to have traveled upward and exited somewhere in the stiff mess of his hair. His clothes are black with blood. He's half wrapped in a bedspread Jack recognizes from past visits to the crooked house, with Hannah. A familiar paring knife is loose near the spare tire.

"I stabbed him. And then he cut me. He put us in the car and took us for a ride out here. I don't know what he was planning to do with us. I don't think he knew. I lost a lot of blood. Which made me dizzy. But. He was bleeding, too, and I don't think he realized how much or how dizzy it made him until I had the gun. And then it just all kind of played out." She stops and says nothing for a while. When she resumes, it's as if she hasn't stopped. "And I had to get the kids to help me put him in here. I didn't want them to, but I was pretty weak. And he was so dead. And I couldn't stand the sight of him. I think my arm is still bleeding. I probably need stitches, but . . ."

Jack nods. Jack closes the trunk. It's still raining. An electric motor takes the lid down the last few inches and locks up, extinguishing the compartment light, leaving everything cold and wet and dark again. Mona waits off to one side, hugging herself, looking out into the pitch-black desert, distractedly. Her hair is slick, soaked.

"Is it the heat that's making him swell up?" she wonders. Jack says nothing, guessing that she isn't really asking a question. "I was thinking, today, maybe I should fill the trunk with ice. They've got an ice machine at the Gas 'N Lube, but I didn't really want to drive his car anywhere. You know." Jack says nothing, waiting, and her voice goes soft again, losing momentum. "I'm scared, Jack."

"Why didn't you just go back to the motel and tell the cops what happened?"

Mona repeats this, flat: "What happened." She turns to look at Jack. "What happened. As if you know what happened. As if you have any idea." The familiar silence falls between them. They just stare at one another.

"Self-defense. We'll go into town, tomorrow, tonight—you decide—and tell the police everything. It's going to be okay."

Mona shakes her head, turns, and starts back up the steps into the house.

Jack calls out to her. "He came after you, he had a gun. You didn't know who he was, I mean, you couldn't know. How could you know? He came after you, you killed him in self-defense."

Mona whirls, angry. "Why did you have to come back here, Jack?"

"Everything's going to be okay."

"Stop saying that!"

"I didn't murder you! I thought maybe Tory had! I came back here, I don't know, to do something about it—"

"You had to clear your name! That's all."

"I came back here because of you! Because of what I thought he did to you!"

Rainwater runs down Mona's face from her hair and Jack can't tell if she's crying, but he suspects she's not. She walks back to where he's standing, looks up into his eyes, then buries her face against his soggy shirt, shaking with despair. He closes his arms around her. Kisses her hair, and then her face when she turns it up to his. Her face, her lips.

"Poor Jack," Mona says desolately. "You're the passerby, the next-door neighbor, the college classmate. No."

"That's what everybody keeps saying," Jack says.

She's very deliberate: "You don't do this part, Jack. You're not the leading man, you're the sidekick. Or the comic relief. Or the sucker."

Jack says, "I've changed."

Mona searches his eyes, kisses him again, then pushes herself out of his arms. She goes up the stairs and back inside, and the door closes, and locks. Jack stands, unmoving, behind the Thunderbird, too stupid or too stubborn to get out of the rain.

"I'm changing," he says again.

Inside the crooked house, Mona enters the bedroom and finds Carrie asleep in the big bed, and Zach at the window, standing on a chair looking out.

"Will he stay out there all night?"

"C'mon, bedtime," Mona says.

The boy hops down. He crawls into a soft, makeshift nest of blankets and sheets Mona has arranged for him in one corner. She tucks him in, presses her nose against his. "You gonna have bad dreams?"

"No." He's lying and she knows it.

"If you get scared, you can come climb in with Carrie and me."

"I'm not scared, Mom."

She stays with him a long time before he closes his eyes.

* * *

Symes lies curled up on the bathroom floor, lit dimly by a spooky plug-in nightlight. Pale and sweaty. He might be feverish. The boots are off. He fumbles weakly with the child-safe cellophane of some pink antacid tablets, has no success liberating a dose, and finally stops when he hears light knocking at the door.

Mona's voice: "You okay?"

"I'm alive," Symes decides, after a moment.

twenty-four

■

It rains all night.

Water washes the desert air of dust and pollen, courses through fissures and creases, phantom gullies and brooks, into one-night creeks that are tributaries to rivers that cut, violent, muddy, roiling, down the sides of barren mountains and across the parched basins of ancient oceans where tomorrow there will be no trace of them.

When the downpour eases into a drizzle, Jack walks out to the edge of the driveway so he can stare up at the bedroom window. Trace dark desert vistas shimmer on the glass. After a moment (but it could have been an hour, or three), Mona's face appears and looks down at him. Then another moment passes and she disappears again.

But Jack waits, because she might come back.

A shattered moon struggles through strings of clouds.

Faraway rumble of thunder. Then nothing.

Then sleep.

* * *

Then Mona.

Bloody. Reeling as if thrown into the wall. Scrambling across the motel room as she flees from Tory Geller. He lunges forward, his dark shape becoming darkness itself.

The sound. Like an effect from a Foley stage, crisp and preternaturally clear. The sound of shovel digging in sandy dirt. Rhythmic. Where is that from? And the paring knife, right in the nightstand drawer. Right where they left it. Limes tumbling to the carpet. The shovel. A pale hand reaches for the paring knife in the drawer. Mona. Up and then down, the arc of the knife, terminating at Jack.

The knife plunges into his heart.

Deep.

No blood.

Jack looks extremely surprised. No blood. Falls backward onto the carpet thick with sloughed-off lives.

Irritated by the inappropriate sound effect of the shovel.

Zach's face is pressed weirdly against the pane of a window. Distorted, nose flat, cheeks flat, lips flat and blooming. Sensible eyes, Mona's eyes. Staring into the front seat of the Thunderbird, where Jack is waking up.

Stiff, shivering in his wet clothes, the sun shining brightly, outside the car port, Jack blinks his dream away. Zach watches him expressionlessly. The shovel sound is persistent and Jack needs to sit up and find out what the hell it is.

His muscles ache, his head aches, his testicles ache. His neck is so stiff he can't turn, so he positions himself to look in the rearview mirror, adjusting it until he can see Symes, out beyond the parking area, in the brush, digging a grave.

The Thunderbird door swings open. Mona holds a bundle of clothes in her arms. "I brought you some dry things." Jack nods, realizes he's too cold to talk. He tries to get out of the car, but his legs are both asleep. Mona helps him. Zach and Carrie stand back, watching their mother help this man walk into the sunlight.

Symes continues to dig.

Mona holds out a sweatshirt Jack recognizes. "That's Tory's."

"I found it in the closet upstairs."

"He didn't like me borrowing his clothes."

"We won't tell him."

Jack can't even get his shirt off, he's too stiff and sore. Can't even get his fingers to work the buttons. Mona does it, avoiding his stare.

"Can I ask you one thing, Jack?"

"Yes."

"What did you do to him?"

"Who?"

"Your friend. I mean, what in the world did you do to him that made him come all the way out here with a gun looking for you?"

"My friend had anger issues."

"Jack."

"I tried to help somebody he was hurting."

Mona stops and searches Jack's eyes, hard. "He said you were f—" she stops herself, remembering her kids. "He said you were sleeping with his wife."

Jack doesn't know how he should respond to this. Mona looks disappointed and unsurprised.

"I didn't believe him," she says after a moment. "I thought he was lying."

"It's more complicated than it sounds."

She says nothing, and finishes unbuttoning his shirt.

"I'm sorry," Jack says.

"You're apologizing to me?"

"You, her, Tory." Jack shivers. "Myself."

"Well, on the plus side, sleeping with your best friend's wife does qualify as a decision, Jack." She moves behind him. "See? You do make them." Jack can't raise his arms. Mona peels his wet shirt off. Jack's ribs and chest are badly bruised. "Oh Jack." Mona shakes her head and looks down at the ground.

"I couldn't get you out of my head," he says finally.

"You ran."

"I did, yeah."

"You don't even know me."

"No, well, maybe—I mean, you're right, but—"

"No more bullshit, Jack. Stop."

Jack takes a step back, in case she's going to slap him again, or kick him. "'Always Faithful.' The tattoo, on your hip."

"What about it?"

"I don't know. You tell me."

"No," she says, with a brittle edge, "you first."

Jack nods. "Maybe it's who you are. Constant. True."

"Semper fidelis?" Mona bites the words off.

"Okay."

"Semper fidelis," Mona repeats bitterly. "It's the fucking Marine Corps motto, Jack. Carrie's father, my last boyfriend, used to get drunk and beat me until I couldn't walk. One day I got this idea, I thought that a tattoo of the Marine Corps motto would prove to him how much I loved him, so that he wouldn't beat me up. You know? I thought, when he got the itch to throw me around, he'd see it, and it would make him stop."

Jack wants to ask whether it worked, but somehow knows it didn't.

"No," Mona says, matter-of-factly, "it didn't work, Jack. I had to shoot him in the head while he was sleeping, to make him stop."

This statement, the casual, cold, and surprisingly satisfied way in which she says it, caroms around in Jack's brain like a ping-pong ball. Shoot him in the head to make him stop. Oh, man.

Mona is quiet for a while. She gives Jack the sweatshirt. "It didn't kill him, but it slowed him down," she adds finally. "I pled to self-defense. I spent some time in jail, and I'm still on probation for it."

Mona smiles sadly. Out at the edge of the driveway, Symes stops shoveling. "Call me cautious, but I don't believe you get two self-defense pleas in one lifetime. So," Mona says, "if I turn myself in, for killing your friend, I'll do hard time this time and they'll put my kids in foster homes. Please don't ask me to do that, Jack. I can't do it. I'm sorry. Not for you, not for anybody. I can't."

Jack stares at her. Then he walks away, numb. Shot him in the head. He walks toward Symes, with no intention of really talking to the man; he just needs somewhere to walk. Halfway there, a barrage of stones hails down on him. He's being carpet bombed by Zach and Carrie.

"Hey! Cut it out! Hey!"

They laugh. Jack lopes in a wide arc to get out of range. He hears Mona scold them, going back inside. The front door opens, and closes.

Symes has finished digging. It's a deep and disciplined rectangular prism, almost shoulder deep. He throws his shovel out, considers the accomplishment of the hole, and then acknowledges Jack.

"Ceviche is raw fish," he says.

"Yes."

"I did not know that." Symes climbs out of the hole. "She explain to you why she can't bail you out of this mess?"

"Carrie's dad."

"Donaldson. He was in my unit back during Desert Storm. What a monumental prick." Symes inspects the calluses on his hands, gouges at one with a thumbnail. "He's at the V.A. in Phoenix sucking disability and weaving lanyards and macramé potholders. Still, that's how I came to know Mona, so I have contradictory feelings about the man. After she popped him, I kept hoping that maybe she and me'd find a common ground. But no, sir. She's had her marine."

Symes takes a deep breath and exhales conclusively. Already moving ahead to the next detail. "I believe I'm gonna need some help here, soon as I freshen up." He walks back to the house.

Jack kicks dirt clods into the hole, listens to the dull percussion, *whup-whadda-wupit*. Goodbye. The secrets are known, the mysteries revealed.

Later, Jack's laying out soggy, bent cigarettes on the trunk of the Thunderbird. One at a time, in a row, on the hot, white metal to dry in the sun. He places each in careful alignment with the others. Primping them if they're crushed. Each is an option, fully formed, precious.

He can hear a vacuum cleaner moving really aggressively across the carpet, somewhere in the house. Footsteps on the gravel. Symes comes down from the front door and across the parking area, washed, his hair wet and combed back like a tilled field. He stops at the car. "There's a double shower in that master bedroom" he says, almost apologetic, "two nozzles, each at an angle, here, and here, soak you from both goddamn sides. And no shower curtain, you just walk around the corner and there it is.

"You ready?" Symes asks.

Jack looks at his perfect row of cigarettes. Depthless shape and shadow, impossible objects, like an Escher illusion. Scoops them up in one soggy mass, and pops open the trunk, ready to get sick or something. But it's not Tory inside. This looks like a scrunched-up wax mannequin wrapped in a bedspread, some misbegotten prop, nothing.

Symes gets leverage on the upper body, gives Jack the impression that maybe he's done this before, and heaves Tory halfway out, so that Jack can get a good grip on the legs, and just like that they're carrying the body away from the open trunk of the Thunderbird, the bedspread dragging.

"What happens after we bury him?" Jack asks.

"What happens?"

"Yeah, after we bury him."

Symes frowns, as if confused. "Specifically involving . . ."

"Mona," Jack says, thinking that Symes is being just a bit of a jerk.

"Oh." Symes tilts his head. "She wants me to go back to the motel in Twentynine Palms and let her mom know she's okay."

Jack is silent.

"She won't go away with you," Symes tells him. "So don't get worked up about that."

They stop at the grave. An awkward moment passes, they're holding this body, Jack's friend, Mona's nightmare, they know what it is that's about to happen, and how it's going to happen, but wish it were, or will be somehow, more graceful. More respectful. Without timing it, or talking, they let go of Tory's corpse at the same moment, it plummets into the hole, and hits bottom with a melon sound.

Symes wipes his hands on his pants unhappily. He takes a gun—the murder weapon, Jack realizes with a jolt—from his back pocket, wipes it off, and tosses it into the grave with the body.

Poor Tory, Jack almost says out loud, without thinking. A line he's said probably a couple dozen times in similar but made-up scenarios, and always as if without thinking about it.

Symes picks up the shovel, and heaves a blade full of dirt into the hole. "You'd of made a shitty soldier, Jack. No offense." He continues burying the body.

"What do you mean she won't go with me?" Jack asks. "And what makes you think that was my plan?"

"She's afraid you'll flake out on her."

"She said that to you?"

"I was pretty surprised myself. It was part of potentially the longest conversation we have ever had." Symes stops, hands the shovel to Jack.

"What else did she say?"

Jack starts to throw loose dirt into the grave. It looked effortless when Symes was doing it, but now Jack is having trouble with the shovel, which is much heavier than he expected, and with the dirt, which is mostly rocks and has Jack wondering how Symes ever dug a hole so deep so quickly. Pretty soon he has to stop.

"You think she's right?" Jack wonders.

"What?"

"What does that mean, do you think?"

"The 'flake' part, or the 'I won't go with him' part?"

Jack hands the shovel back, frustrated. "What the fuck am I supposed to do? What does she want from me?"

"Ask her."

"I'm asking you."

"I don't even like you."

"I know."

Symes seems to think he's said all he needs to say. Jack shakes his head. "I can only see out of one eye, Symes."

"And."

"Depth of field. You know. I have, what—no sense of perspective."

"I'm bad with math."

"It's not math."

Symes leans on the shovel, contemplative. "You know how there's all these stories about the cowardly guy who falls on the grenade to save his unit? And because he falls on the grenade, everybody realizes he wasn't a coward at all?"

"Yeah, okay. I thought that was just something in, you know," Jack practically winces as he says it, "movies."

"No."

"I'm kidding."

Symes starts shoveling dirt into the grave again. "You don't hear about it so much anymore. What with IEDs and so forth, suicide bombers, giving an individual no real time to react. I mean, jihad. And whatnot. New rules. But still. Soldier did it just last month in Helmand Province. Outside of Musa Qaleh. You probably heard about it."

Jack just stares at him.

"It's a state of mind," Symes adds.

Jack doesn't like where this is going. "But he's dead."

"Who?"

"The company coward. Or whoever. He leaps on the grenade, and yeah, maybe he's not a coward anymore, but he's dead."

"Okay."

"He's dead," Jack repeats, with a different emphasis.

"I'm not saying it's for everyone," Symes agrees, and continues burying Tory.

Jack looks out across the drying desert. It's an indefinite horizon, undistinguished, brown bleeding into blue. Rocks, again, are pelting him. Carrie and Zach. He looks over to the high ground where they're dug in behind the manzanita. They're smiling at him, smiling and throwing rocks.

He remembers Tory telling him, "It comes down to one thing, and one thing only," assuming Jack knew what that one thing was.

He does. It turns out, he does.

He finds himself moving down the driveway. Walking fast. After a moment, he starts to run, away, down-slope, skidding awkwardly on the loose stones, arms windmilling for balance.

He hears Symes say "Hey!" then is only aware of the blood pumping past his ears, but gravity is pulling him downhill, and it feels pretty good to be moving.

In the crooked house, Mona is vacuuming the glass from the shattered door, wrestling with attachments when Zach bursts in, tracking mud across the carpet.

"The man is leaving!" he says.

The vacuum roars. "Mommy can't hear you when she's vacuuming."

"The man is leaving!" Zach shouts.

Mona turns off the vacuum cleaner. Zach is wide-eyed, victorious, scared, confused.

"The man is leaving! We threw rocks at him and he's leaving!"

Mona runs out.

Down in the blackbrush near the county road, Jack guns the engine of the Bonneville and its tires spit mud. The big car rocks back and forth, trying to free itself from the soft desert soil. He hears voices, looks in the side mirror.

Mona is running down the driveway from the house, as fast as she can. Jack can see Symes, farther back, with the children, watching from the parking area.

"Jack!" Mona shouts.

The Bonneville fishtails forward, then reverses backward out of the brush, across the rain-softened driveway, flattening a swath of mesquite on the other side. He glances up the driveway, again, at Mona, racing toward him.

"JACK!"

Jack does his best star-turn smile, and the car whipsaws out of the driveway and onto the county road. He careens in and then out of a washout, bottoms out and scrapes the muffler, and points the car south.

Mona stops running when she gets to the road. But she stands watching the Bonneville disappear over rise after rise in the unpaved roadway, long after dust and distance make it pointless to watch anymore.

twenty-five

■

Driving up, Jack can see, through the big glass front doors of the Twentynine Palms police station, the main desk and the one, often-bored receptionist behind it, reading a paperback novel she can finish by Friday, if things don't get too busy.

He passes a mural on the wall of a Christian bookstore, a trompe l'oeil of an artist who apparently fell asleep while he was painting the mural. It's a skilled piece of work, because the man on the scaffold and the bull just below him look three-dimensional when compared to the unfinished mural behind them. The painted shadows sell it, and Jack, in a glance, is convinced that what he's seen is real. He'll think about it for a long time, when he remembers this last day in Twentynine Palms: the odd still life of a sleeping painter and the conundrum of the shorthorn bull loose in the parking lot.

Jack's Bonneville pulls up next to the front door, parks illegally. Jack gets out and goes inside as another cop is leaving; it's Petty, and Jack says a convivial hello.

Petty stops, does a double take. The slow turn.

And Jack hits him.

It's the first time in his life that Jack has hit anyone, but there are a lot of intangibles behind it (all those fake fights and phantom punches thrown, all that idle braggadocio from stunt men between takes), and with a beginner's luck it lands just right on the side of Petty's face, rocking him almost comically off his feet, lights out, folding back, arms spread, London Bridge, falling.

Down.

And out, apparently, because the park service man doesn't move, and after a wary moment Jack comes up from the somewhat defensive crouch he took after delivering the sucker punch, when he was still anticipating some kind of response from the cop.

But no. Petty is down, and out.

The receptionist inside is standing, mouth gaped in an astonished O, frozen as Jack enters and amiably asks her his question. She doesn't hesitate, and quickly hurries back into the station, while Jack waits, rubbing some feeling back into his hand, and Petty stays down. Jack looks out at him again and smiles his easy, near-star smile.

Hardly any time elapses before Deputy Ng comes out to the front desk with the receptionist. He recognizes Jack immediately and tries a little too hard not to act surprised to see him, but his attention is split between Jack and Petty, belly-up on the sidewalk, just outside the front door. And while Jack is talking, beginning to explain something in elaborate detail, gesturing, animated, a full performance, Ng is doing the necessary calculations, gauging this apparent assault on a police officer against that unprovoked beating the park service cop bragged he whupped up on Jack in the jail cell, enabling Ng to make a spot decision that, yes, maybe there is cosmic justice, and, heck, maybe Petty just tripped over the threshold on his way out, and communicating all of this to Jack, while Jack's talking, with a neutral expression, an emphatic indifference to Petty's demise.

Eventually Soles comes out from the squad room with a couple other uniformed cops, and, to be sure, nobody seems to care that Petty is down, and everyone stays quiet, listening, fairly astounded, as Jack tells his tale.

twenty-six

■

Zach is in the window of the crooked house, watching police cars come up the driveway.

The Crown Vics park, willy-nilly, radios bleating static and dispatch, springs sighing as the officers emerge. Leather holsters and belts and gear actually squeak. Symes appears behind Zach and folds his arms, looking down. Jack gets out of the backseat of one of the cars, flanked quickly by Ng and Soles. Their shadows jitter and twine on the sloping desert aggregate as he leads them to the place where Tory Geller is freshly buried. It's late in the afternoon. Heat ghosts from the sun-baked terrain.

Mona opens the front door. She's holding Carrie. Shading her eyes from the low sun, she stands pretty much motionless, looking down at Jack, who finally glances up at her without expression, then never looks back at her again.

epilogue

■

a.

A low-tar cigarette.

Ash up, half burned.

Smoke curls from the glowing embers.

Jack Baylor, in a slate-colored, one-piece poly-blend jumpsuit typical of the California state correctional system, sits at a metal desk bolted to the floor of his solitary cell in a small, minimum-security work-farm facility somewhere deep in the Imperial Valley, unwrapping a cardboard mailing tube addressed to him.

He tilts back, his chair squeaks, he retrieves the cigarette between his thumb and forefinger and puts it between his lips. He pulls out a rolled piece of canvas. Two squares of colored paper flutter free. A tiny MP3 player drops onto the desk.

He picks up the two pieces of paper.

One offers a scribbled, multicolored mass of felt pens and passion, signed "Carrie." The other is a simple square-ish drawing of a man getting pelted by rocks.

b.

The Roundup Room is empty, of course, except for Mona and the bartender. Mona is drinking Maker's Mark. Blue dress, blue pumps.

"Then what happens?" It's the bartender asking the questions, he really wants to know, it's not just bartender etiquette.

"I don't remember," Mona tells him. "I kind of lost interest after Jack's scene, where he plays the priest."

"I saw the trailer. Looked seriously lame."

"You don't go to movies, though."

"No. I watch the trailers. You can see them online."

"Everything looks lame online."

"Well, okay, fair enough. But—" He gestures vaguely. "Still. The trailers suffice for me."

The arched eyebrow, the sly, slow smile: "Suffice?"

The front door opens—there's a new cowbell on it that clingle-clangs, rowdy. Symes strides in. Same old gunner wearing Jack's Larry Mahan boots. Mona whistles at him. Symes turns red, sits down at the bar, careful to leave one stool between them.

Mona's surprised, pleased, that he's wearing the boots. Symes explains dryly that he promised to keep them broken in, as if it were a military mission. Mona doesn't miss this tone in his delivery.

"Marines," she tells the bartender.

"Semper fi," the bartender replies.

Symes sits stiffly. He tells them, "That's right," not about to be busted for twenty-five years of honorable service to God and country.

Mona smiles, and asks him again if he's sure he wants to go through with this.

Symes answers that he said he would and so he will. He told

Jack that he would, so he will. Symes punctuates this with a proud, Quantico frown. There's nothing more to say. He doesn't move from his seat though, not yet. Cubes drop and clatter in the automatic icemaker under the bar. Neon hums. The bartender puts a low glass out for Symes, and pours him a finger of bourbon.

Mona says, as if indifferently, that it's not like she's waiting for him.

Symes knows she means Jack, and knows that she's lying, but goes along with it, and pretends that Jack knows she's not waiting and has no expectations.

Eighteen months, Mona says, sadly optimistic.

Or maybe less, is Symes' opinion. Depends.

Maybe less.

Symes tells her simply that it's like a deployment, but with nobody shooting at him.

Samba music blasts on the stereo. Classic Clementina de Jesus. "Incompatibilidade de Genios." Mona drains her drink and slides off her stool. She puts her hand out, waiting.

c.

Dead center in his tiny cell, Jack unfurls the canvas roll he received in the mail, revealing a big schematic of painted footsteps and arrows, and the words "Basic Samba." He puts on the mini-headphones, and adjusts them over his ears. Then he plugs them into the cheap Chinese MP3 stick, and clicks Play.

A cold, dull, concrete stillness folds over Jack's cell, but inside the man is moving, struggling to keep pace with the rhythm in his headphones, his feet dancing over the printed footprints on the floor map.

Arms out, up, poised, embracing his imaginary partner.

d.

And Rachel.

She's at her desk, doing math homework under protest.

This is probably sometime in February of her junior year. Her grades are good and she's starting to think about college, maybe back East, although the weather will be an issue. There's a boyfriend, but it's not serious. She's not into anime anymore, and Hello Kitty has given ground to Murakami, but her collection of high-tops has grown to over a dozen, and she flew to Paris with just her dad last spring, a surprise vacation, and it was probably her second-best trip ever. She's grown into her body. Her eyes no longer have that buoyantly bright, piercing indifference of the blissfully adolescent girl, but she still carries herself with confidence, even if Trig is her worst subject, and Mr. Davis is a dickweed.

Her laptop computer screen glows with Twitter, Facebook, and several overlapping instant messaging conversations, boxed narratives in a mostly gibberish haiku. Ihartxcountrymor, PinkUnicizorn233, mugggsaBlather, mranonymous27.

Her bulletin board is covered with pictures.

One of them is familiar.

A faded old snapshot of Jack Baylor, misty dream guy of a Rincon Beach summer day, he's slender in his wetsuit, coming out of a roiling surf, smiling, and forever seventeen.

acknowledgements

■

Marty Bauer, Robert Bookman, and Eric Lax for their early encouragement. Simon Green for his invaluable wisdom and guidance. Charlie Winton for believing in it; Julie Pinkerton for believing in it draft after draft. And Erich Anderson, who inspired it, urged me to pursue it, and without whose unflagging friendship and optimism and backseat driving I would never have finished it.

Twentynine Palms is a very real place in the high desert, stark and beautiful, and I hope it will not begrudge me the literary license I have taken in this work of fiction.